EAST of the Sun, WEST of the Moon

"Jackie Morris has updated and re-imagined the
tale of *East of the Sun And West of the Moon* for a
new generation of readers, upsetting the boundaries
of happy endings and asserting that heroines are
not obligated to move in expected patterns."
Robin Hobb

"Combining an acute eye for the majesty of nature
with a gorgeous palette and a poet's vision,
Jackie Morris creates magic with
every stroke of her brush."
Jane Johnson

For Hannah Stowe and Erin Keen,
with love.

JANETTA OTTER-BARRY BOOKS

First published in Great Britain and in the USA in 2013 by
Frances Lincoln Children's Books, 4 Torriano Mews,
Torriano Avenue, London NW5 2RZ
www.franceslincoln.com

ISBN 978-1-84780-294-1

Illustrated with watercolour
Set in ITC Veljovic LT

Printed in China by C&C Offset Printing Co. Ltd in Nov 2012
1 3 5 7 9 8 6 4 2

EAST of the Sun, WEST of the Moon

JACKIE MORRIS

F

FRANCES LINCOLN
CHILDREN'S BOOKS

In an iridescent sparkle of frosted light he appeared, a huge white bear, shifting and shimmering into solid form. Frost stars clung to his thick pelt. He shook himself and they danced around him like an echo of the Northern Lights.

Noise and lights and smells, hurrying people, sirens, car horns and engines. People rushed by, coat collars high against the cold, and only the child in a pushchair saw and gasped, pointing at the white bear in the dark city street.

He sniffed the city air deep into his black nose. Car fumes, perfume, sweat and oil, metal, rubber, rotting vegetables, cigarette smoke, winter – and beneath it all the faintest trace of 'her'. She had walked here earlier.

He shook his giant head as if to shake the noise out of it and followed the stream of scent that was her, moving fast through the scurrying crowds. A ghost of a bear, unseen by the busy busy people, passing cars, buses and bikes, people on their way home from work, others on their way to work, people huddled in sleeping bags in shop doorways. He moved towards the edge of the city, past prostitutes in short skirts and huge coats, and the slow-cruising cars, past the huddled dealers of drugs on corners of parks and streets.

As he came out from the streets of shops towards the houses and flats, he stopped to sniff deeply again. In a doorway, down a dark alley he saw a child, no more than twelve, huddled in a bundle of blankets. Beside her was a cup and a sign that simply said "Please". He felt what she felt: lost, lonely and afraid, stone-cold and balanced on the edge of life and death. She saw him as a flickering image – a memory, a wish, something half-remembered from a story in another life.

He caught the scent of the one he searched for and set off at a run down the street away from the shops. But first he moved closer to the child and breathed on her, and she felt the bear's hot, fishy breath wash through her with a healing warmth, even to her frozen fingers. Then he breathed into the cup. As he lumbered away into the night she watched, amazed. She picked up the cup. It was heavy with gold.

The girl stood by the window and watched the beginning of the snow falling. She was cold and tired. She pulled the blanket round her a little tighter and went to help her sister with the fire.

This evening they would have a feast. After school she had gone with her brother round the market stalls as they were closing up, packing away boxes into the backs of vans. Fruit and vegetables too ripe to sell another day were thrown away or left by the side of the road. They had collected enough for a good meal, and the old lady who kept the wholefoods stall had slyly given her a bag with rice and bulgar and even, she discovered when she unpacked the bag later, a small bag of fruit sweets.

Behind the supermarket they had dodged the security guards to go through the skips for out-of-date bread and frozen foods. And so they came home with quite a hoard. Now it was quiet in the flat and the smell of stew made it seem almost homely.

They had been poor even before they came to this country: she and her father, mother and three brothers and three sisters. Her father wrote for a newspaper, and when she was young their lives had been good. But then the government had changed and their father wrote things that the new rulers did not like.

They had come for him one night. A knock on the door – then they burst into the house and dragged him away. Days later they brought him back, broken and bruised with threats of what would happen to his wife, to his children, if he continued to write. So they had fled, a frightening journey over land and sea, to claim asylum in this new country.

Yet things were little better here. They were treated as criminals 'while their case was investigated'. Over and over, her father was interrogated about his torture at the hands of the government, was forced to relive the horror and humiliation until he sank into despair. Unable to work, feed or clothe the family, they lived off charity, little more than beggars.

Their journey to the new land had been terrifying. They had placed themselves in the hands of people-traffickers, afraid of discovery, death, separation. Now they lived with the fear of being returned to their homeland to certain death, and with the dread of their children being taken away by the government in this new country.

At school she had no friends. The other children were frightened by the haunted, far-away look in her eyes.

But tonight they could pretend things were normal. The smells of cooking filled every corner of the room, and her mother sang as she stirred the pot.

The knock at the door brought back all their fears. Was it the police, come to take them away, to send them back?

Father walked to the door and drew back the bolts.

Outside, the white bear shimmered in the orange street-lights. He swayed gently from side to side, and his white-mist breath blurred the frosted air. "I searched for you from afar," he said, his voice slow and gravelly, but in their native tongue. "May I come in?"

As if enchanted, her father stepped back, and the great bear came into their home. He shook his coat and it sparkled with frost. His white fur carried the dark marks of his trek through the city streets.

From the first moment she saw him, the girl knew that the bear had come for her. How many times had she dreamt of him, of riding on his back, sleeping, wrapped safe in his paws, walking beside him? How many times, on their terrifying journey, had she imagined the bear walking beside her, guarding her family while they slept? Now he was here, as if spelled from her dreams.

He lay down before her, head on his giant paws, snow stars caught in his white white fur. "Forgive me," he growled, "but I need you. Only come away with me and your family will be well and all manner of things will be well. This I promise you."

Her mother's hand was at her mouth. Father stepped between the girl and the bear.

But in the eyes of the bear she thought she could see tears like frozen diamonds, and through to his soul, a depth of sadness beyond her understanding.

It seemed to the others that time had stopped, but then the girl took her father's hand and knelt before the bear. She reached out with her other hand to touch the bear's face, stroking his fur, which felt damp and thick and warm, so warm on her fingers. As she moved her hand over his face his eyes closed. He seemed almost to smile and a great sigh shook him. He smelled of the forests, of wildness and of home. From the first touch of fingertips on fur she knew she had no choice.

"I will come with you, Bear," she said.

But her family all cried out at once. "NO."

Confusion fell upon the house, and then her father spoke. "How can this be? Here in this city, in the twenty-first century, a talking bear walks into our house? We do not live in fairy tales, we do not live in stories. And he says you must go and all will be well.

Go where? For what? What will he do? Tear you apart and eat you? And what will we do without you? Have we been through so much together to lose you now?"

By his side, her mother had sunk to her knees and was crying, swaying a little while the others clung to her.

The girl cupped the great bear's head in her hands, and breathed his warmth to give her courage. She must go with him.

"I will come back in a week," he softly said. "Be ready. Bring only what you need." With that he was gone, out into the night with its orange lights and distant siren sounds, leaving behind the faintest trace of the forest smell of home.

For a week they argued. They would lock her in, send her away, move away themselves, but to where? There was nowhere they could go. They would go to the police, and tell them what? That a talking bear had come into their house and threatened to take away their oldest child. The police would think them mad. They began to think they *were* mad, that they had had some kind of collective nightmare. But the girl knew the truth, and when a week had passed she collected into a bundle the few things she would take.

There was a knock on the door. The girl drew back the bolts and there stood the bear. He swayed gently from side to side, bowed his head to her and waited.

To all her brothers and sisters she gave a hug and a kiss, holding the smallest so tightly. Her mother tried to turn away but she took her face in her hands and kissed her. She said, "Forgive me. You know that I have to do this."

And to her father she said, "I love you. Look after them all." She wiped a tear from his ragged face with her soft hand.

The bear knelt and she climbed astride his huge back. Then they were gone.

They moved through the city like a shimmer, like a whisper. Past the blur of lights and the smudge of noise and out into the snow-covered countryside.

Her hair flew out behind her as they moved over the hills and far away. On the back of the bear she swayed to his rhythm, hands pushed deep into his shaggy coat, and the warmth of him spread from her fingers to her toes.

They came to a rise, a conical hill covered in tall trees, black bones against the winter sky.

For a moment the bear paused. "Are you afraid?" His question wandered through the trees as, far below, the city of tiny lights sparkled, orange stars in the deep, dark valley.

"No," she answered. She wasn't. For he was the guardian bear of her dreaming. Over the past few months and years fear had been burnt out of her – fear for her father, her family, fear of all the strangeness of this new unwelcoming place where they sought only refuge. With the bear, for reasons beyond her understanding, it was not fear she felt but hope.

On they went, and the sway of his running lulled her mind and rocked her body until she felt she had passed into a dream, and soon she would wake and be back in her bed at home in her own country.

Then she jarred into wakefulness and wondered at the mystery of riding the great white bear through a foreign land. Church clocks chimed around them: one o'clock, two o'clock, three o'clock, four. They came to a stop at the edge of a high, wide cliff. Below, only the sea and its lacy edge of waves against a rocky shore.

"Are you afraid?" rumbled the bear's deep voice.

No, she wasn't.

"Hold tight," he said, and they leapt from the top of the cliff, over the sea, and her heart flew to her mouth. Then they were riding across the night sky on a silver bridge of stars, and her heart and soul lifted for the joy and beauty of it all. High in the sky, the bone-white moon shone down on the girl, the bear and the sea of cloud.

How long they travelled she had no idea. At times she slept, and even waking she seemed in a dream. But at last they dropped down to earth again, to a land of

snow and mountains. Amongst the thick forest trees, arctic foxes, ptarmigan and snow-shoe hares moved silently, hushed by the snow. White owls called, and in the distance she could hear the music of wolves praising the beauty of the cold, stone-white moon.

They went on, over the snow, through the tall forest, to a wall of rock that seemed to rise into the stars.

Again the bear stopped. "Are you afraid?" For the third time he asked, and for the third time, "No," she answered. "Should I be afraid of you?"

She placed her hand on the bear's great head, gently stroked his ears, and for a moment it seemed that the deep sadness was lifted from his coal-black eyes and there was the faintest hint of a smile.

For an answer the bear only grunted and walked to the stone face of a cliff, which she could see now was traced with thick leaf patterns of frost. Three times he breathed his hot, bear breath on the wall and, as she watched, the frost patterns melted and flowed and changed and resolved themselves into the shape of a door, richly decorated with animals and birds of the forest. Deer, martin, wolf and fox.

A push from the bear's paw and the door opened wide into a beautiful hallway aglow with candles, shining in the light of a thousand flowers of dancing flame. They stepped inside and behind her the door swung shut.

She followed the bear down hallways, through rooms lit with candles, in elegant lanterns shaped like birds, whose flickering flames made the shadow wings fly and dance around the walls. Deeper and deeper they went, into the heart of the bear's lair.

They came at last to a room where a fire burned, like a warm flower in a fireplace. At the end of this room a table was laid out with fruit and bread and a warm stew. She sat and ate while the bear watched and waited.

Weary now even to her bones, she gathered up cushions and lay in front of the fire, and slept and dreamt of a long long journey, of a bridge of silver stars across a deep, dark sky and of a warm fire.

The bear lay and watched her sleeping by the fire, and his eyes again filled with diamond tears. So beautiful she looked sleeping there. So young.

She slept for a long time and woke in a huge, curtained bed. Slowly she gathered her memories to her. She stretched away the night of sleep, the stiffness from the long ride, and climbed down from the high bed to a table set for breakfast. A bowl of deep-red cherries, peaches and plums with a heady smell of summer, a jug of warm milk and another of cream, a loaf, fresh from the oven and crisp-crusted, and a steaming pot of aromatic tea.

Beside her bed she found her bundle. In a wardrobe she discovered a long red gown, simple but elegant. She dressed, then set off to explore.

The bear's castle was huge, corridor after corridor, room after room, each beautifully decorated with wonderful furniture. There were music rooms and living rooms, a map room, a library, a room with a ceiling of stars and moons and a telescope. There was a garden room with orchids and heavy-scented lilies where tiny, jewel-like birds flew among the plants, and butterflies came to rest in her hair. She found a bathing room with a bath like a pool, decorated with tiles, all portraying different animals, birds and fish in colours that glowed.

All day she wandered through the marvellous palace, and just when she realised she was hungry and began to wonder if she would ever find her way back through the maze of rooms, there was the bear, quietly watching and waiting for her.

"You slept well?" he said.

"Thank you, I did."

"And your breakfast? It was as you would have wished?"

"Yes. Thank you."

"But now you are hungry again. Follow me." And he led her down a new corridor.

Soon they came to a small room where a table was

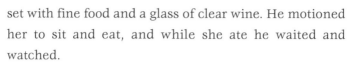

set with fine food and a glass of clear wine. He motioned her to sit and eat, and while she ate he waited and watched.

"Why did you bring me here?" she asked the white bear.

"I cannot say. I can tell you only that I searched for you for many years. That you had to come to me of your own free will. That if you did, I could promise that for you and your family all would be well and all manner of things would be well. My house is your house. If you want anything, need anything, only ring this silver bell and you shall have it."

On the table in front of her she saw a small silver bell threaded with a ribbon. The silver was traced with delicate birds, like the tiny jewel birds in the garden room.

She tied the ribbon round her neck and walked over to where the bear lay. She knelt down in front of him, reached out her hand to touch his face, and the bear flinched away from the warmth of her hand. As she ran her hand down his ear to his great shaggy mane he seemed to sigh and shake a little. His dark eyes showed a weight of sadness and he turned his head away from her.

"Have you eaten enough?" he asked.

"Thank you, yes."

"Then follow." He led her back to her bedchamber where the bed was made and the lights burned low. "You must rest now." And with that he was gone. As he moved swiftly along the hallway the lights dimmed, leaving only a tunnel of darkness where the bear had been.

On the bed she found a white lace nightgown, long and heavy, smelling of meadowsweet and honeysuckle, and a book. She put on the nightgown, put the bell by her bedside and climbed into the high bed with its soft pillows and brilliant white linen sheets. Weary now, she blew out the candle and lay back. The dark room creaked and settled into the night, and on the very edge of her hearing she thought she heard the distant howling of a wolf singing its wild song to the moon. Almost before her head touched the pillow she sank into a deep sleep.

She woke suddenly as her door clicked open. It was dark. The deep darkness of a tunnel at night-time. Fear prickled her skin. She felt a shiver, like a cold finger, trace her spine. She kept her breathing shallow, felt her heart beat fast and loud as a drum beat while her ears struggled to catch every sound.

Someone, or something, stepped across the floor of the room and moved around her bed. It pulled back the covers and climbed in, next to her. She felt, rather than heard, it rest its head on the pillow and relax into sleep, then a quiet, rhythmic breathing.

She waited, still as stone, listening to the thing beside her sleep, not daring to move in case she woke it, hardly daring to breath. When she was sure it was in a deep sleep she reached across to the lantern by her bed and tried to light the candle. But try as she might, she could not get a match to light, not even to spark.

For a long while she lay awake and listened. Not heavy enough, not large enough to be the bear, but someone or something was there. After a while and despite her fear, she sank into a troubled sleep.

In the morning when she woke, her fear returned.

She was alone in the huge bed. Whoever or whatever it was had risen without waking her and gone. She wondered if she had dreamt it, but no, the pillows bore the imprint of someone, something, and the covers were crumpled. More curious now than frightened, as the room was filled with light, she waited for the bear to find her. Yet when he came she found that she could not ask him about her night-time visitor, though she was not able to say why.

And so her days and nights passed and rolled into weeks and months, and she lived in the enchanted place with the bear. Each afternoon she would turn from whatever she was doing to see the bear standing, watching. Together they would go to the library and she would take down a book and read aloud. After a few days she would gather up a pile of cushions from the chairs and, sitting on the floor, would lean her back against the bear, pillowing her head in his heavy white pelt. He would listen as she read him tales of magic and enchantment, of heroes and witches, dragons and knights, kings and castles.

Sometimes she would find herself lulled by his

steady breathing, the warmth of his coat and the gentle musky smell of bear. She would drift into sleep and dream of a prince, young and handsome. She would wake to find her head cradled on his great paw, body curled close into him as he waited for her to wake and read on. She would reach up and run her hand along the silky short hair of his brow and he would purr like a great cat. But always at the back of his eyes there was a shadow of sadness, a well of longing.

Each morning she woke to a breakfast of the freshest, juiciest fruit. Each afternoon she would read to the bear. Food appeared as if by magic. She saw no one but the bear. If she wanted a bath she would find that it was filled and ready for her with water of just the right temperature, lavender-scented.

Each day fresh flowers would greet her waking. Each night she would find a perfect red rose on her pillow. If there was anything she wanted she had only to ring the bell.

And every night, just after she had blown out her light ready for sleep, someone or something would come into her room, tiptoe around the bed and climb in next to her, rest its head on the pillow and sleep. She was never able to light a candle to see who it was. She could not bring herself to reach across the bed to touch, to seek for a clue. And never, next day, did she ask the bear who her night-time visitor might be. But with each night that passed her curiosity grew.

For the most part she was happy, happier than she had been since her childhood ended in a rage of fear and violence.

She had few desires. Almost everything she wanted could be found in her enchanted home. But she missed the silky feel of a fresh breeze on her skin, the kiss of rain, the smell of the air before a snowfall and the song of birds. There were no windows in the bear's home.

Most of all she missed her family. She thought of them often, in quiet moments, and once, when she was holding the silver bell, she remembered with longing the photographs of her growing up.... When her family fled they had taken few things, only those most precious. She had chosen an album of photographs. Inside were pictures of her mother and father when they were other people – not yet her mother, not yet her father, but young and carefree. Just two young people falling in love, then holding hands on their wedding day.

Through the pages she could trace the life of her family, each time a new child was added, and each face carried a resemblance, an echo of the others. Her favourite photograph was a casual moment of peace and happiness snapped from their lives, huddled close together so that they all fitted in the frame, smiling. She would look at it and see her own small child's face smiling back through time at her.

But in all the confusion of their journey the album had been lost.

The next morning when she woke, there on the bedside table beside the candle, was the photograph in a silver frame. She held it close, her breath misting the glass as she touched each face with the tip of her finger, and tears began to flow.

Hours later the bear found her, sobbing gently,

holding the photo to her heart. With his rough bear's tongue he licked away her salty tears and pushed his head into her lap. "I thought it would make you happy," he growled. "Did you not wish for this with the silver bell?"

"Oh, Bear, it does make me happy. But how I miss them. I have everything I could want. You are so kind. But I miss them so. And I long to tell them I am well, to see my father smile again, to hear my mother's voice."

With a deep rumble of a sigh the bear said, "Do you want this so very much?"

"I do."

He growled deep and dangerous and pulled away from her, paced around the room, clumsy and huge now. He stood and swayed from side to side, from foot to foot, swinging his great head. Seeing him so, she began to fear him. In their time together he had always been a gentle companion. Now he was animal, and she felt the danger of wildness that spun around him.

It was only a moment. Then he calmed and said, "If this is what you wish, I will have to let you go. You may visit your family for a month and a day. I will take you." His voice cracked a little as he spoke. "But you must beware. I ask you only one thing. You must never allow yourself to be alone with your mother. She loves you. Wants only what she thinks is best for you... but she will try to hold you, and if you are alone with her great harm will come from it. Do you understand?"

The girl heard only that she would see her family again. For a month and a day she would be back with them.

"You will come back to me?" The bear's voice was almost a whisper.

"Yes, oh yes. Thank you, I will. When can I go?"

"Tomorrow. In the morning."

And with that he was gone.

She fell backwards, fast, tumbling, as if falling in a dream to wakefulness. She opened her eyes in panic and her mind caught up with her body. She felt the bear's warm strength beneath her and looked around and it was then that she realised he must have made a mistake.

From one fairytale palace they had travelled through time and space to another. Around them was a parkland, coated with snow made pink by light reflected from the early morning sun. A wide, double avenue of trees led away in either direction, as far as the eye could see.

As the girl and the bear appeared on the path between the trees, the sky filled with the clamour and swirl of a thousand rooks, startled from their roosts in the skeletal branches.

"You will come back to me?" She could hardly hear the bear's voice as it mingled with those of the rooks.

"Yes," she whispered. "I will." She held tight, twisting her fingers into his pelt, which still carried the iridescent dust of their journey.

Slowly he walked along the majestic avenue.

At first the house looked like a doll's house. But as they came closer she began to realise it was huge, a palace fit for a prince, with gardens laid out, short hedges woven in knots and patterns, all made white with the covering of snow. There were arches which promised roses in spring, hidden gardens and walled gardens.

Near the house were paddocks where horses pawed the snow with neat hooves to find the grass beneath, breath floating like dragon smoke from their wide velvet nostrils. When they scented the bear their heads lifted and, seeing him, they shied and galloped, kicking and bucking, dancing in the showers of snow they kicked up.

She began to get anxious. This was nothing like home. Doubt nibbled at the furthest corners of her mind. Had he tricked her? Had he never meant to take her home to her family? Was this some kind of test?

"Where are you taking me, Bear?" she asked.

And he answered, "To those you want to see most in the world."

They passed the sweep of steps that led to the tall black door. Peacocks, brilliant blue, stamped at the snow. Around the side of the house there were cottages, blind windows reflecting the white parkland, and at one window a small miracle. The face of a child, blurred behind the steam of breath, eyes made brighter by the light of snow.

She felt her heart lift at the sight of her brother, and at the same time she felt the bear retreat into himself.

Two hands pressed against the cold glass. They wiped, he pressed his nose hard against the window and then there was a muffled shout as he pulled away Seconds later they all spilled out of the door, in pyjamas and thick dressing gowns, slippered feet crunching the snow. They scooped her up into their arms, held her back at arms' length, looked her over to pull her back and hold her close and never, never let her go again. And there were smiles and laughter and tears.

As they pulled her towards the door she remembered the bear and turned to thank him. He stood a little way off, head down, watching.

"I'll come inside, in a moment. I must say goodbye to the bear."

And one by one they peeled away into the warmth of the house. Her father went last and held on to her hand, but she pushed him gently towards the door.

"Just a minute," she said, "then I will be with you."

He turned reluctantly and left them alone, outside.

The bear walked slowly to stand before her and she knelt in the cold snow. He shook himself, from his nose all along his body, as if to shake off the melancholy that was settling on him. It seemed that the Northern Lights shone around him again.

"You will remember?" he said. "Do not be alone with your mother. All will be lost if you listen to her. I will come back in a month and a day. You will come home with me?"

The last was a question, not an order.

She reached up her hand as far as she could until she felt the thickest, richest fur behind the bear's ears and pulled his head towards her. She rested her head against his. "Thank you, Bear." And she kissed him gently.

His sigh was like the wind in the trees.

She ran her hands down the sides of his long head, to the end of his muzzle, and he licked her hand. Deep in his eyes hope softened the sadness. Then he turned and was gone.

She felt in her heart a lurch, a catch. Her breath was shallow and her hand was shaking. At the edge of her hearing she heard a distant roar like thunder. Was it pain or loneliness? She put her hand to her cheek, where the bear had kissed it, and felt a flush of colour rise to her face. Then she heard her family calling, and she turned away into the warmth of the house, leaving the birds to gossip and settle in the black branches.

They were gathered round a huge oak table in a warm kitchen that smelled of toast and strong coffee. The smell took her straight back to the happy days of childhood, before their troubles began. It was so long since their home had been like this, she had almost forgotten.

Mother busied herself with plates and knives, butter

and bustle, while the others threw questions at her from all directions, until her father held up his hands and called for calm.

And so they sat down to breakfast. Thick toast and honey and fruit. Mother poured her a cup of coffee and as she sipped at its bitterness she knew it was a mark of her growing up.

Slowly she told her story, of her gentle days with the bear, how she was happy, but missed them. How she was safe. How he treated her with great kindness. But she did not tell them of the night-times and the strange visitor to her room.

And she wanted to know how they came to be here, in this warm and cosy cottage by the huge house. As she finished her story she sat back and looked round the table. Their faces had lost the sharpness of hunger and fear. Now they were well clothed, and there was colour in their cheeks. Even her father's eyes wore less of the haunted echo of despair.

Her mother and the children cleared away the breakfast things while her father sat by her side, just holding her hand, touching her face as if to check that she was really there.

Then they told her how, the day after she had gone, there was another knock on the door. No bear this time, but a woman. She had introduced herself, a lawyer, from an organisation called Human Rights First. She had been working on a case with other refugees when she had come across their file.

She had recognised their father's name and was horrified to find that, despite all they had been through, they had been treated so brutally in this new country. His work had been much admired among her colleagues and when he disappeared it was feared that he had died. Now she had found him she wanted to help, to highlight his work, and their case, and to offer them help in any way she could.

Within days she had talked to the owner of a national newspaper, a rich and powerful woman with friends in government. A few days later their visa was pushed through, temporary, but still a visa. It recognised their status as refugees, gave them back a little of their pride, but most of all entitled her father to work again. He was offered a job at the newspaper and a cottage for his family next to the owner's house. She lived alone in the huge mansion and said that she would welcome the noise of a young family.

Now the children went to the local school, and had the run of the house and grounds. Father found some healing with the opportunity to write again. His work was becoming well known. They had food, money, warm clothes, a sense of security and self-respect. They worked to help the organisation that had so changed their lives, her father through his journalism, her mother as an interpreter, helping others like themselves to find peace in this new place.

She remembered the words of the bear, that if she went with him, 'all would be well and all manner of things would be well'. Had he made all this happen?

As their story finished, Mother shooed them all away to their rooms to get dressed, and she went too, aware that the bear had warned her not to be alone with her mother. A curious warning that her mother would do them harm. Anyway, her sisters wanted to show her something.

Upstairs they led her to a room and threw open

the door. It was beautiful, cosy, with pillows piled high and books in their new language and the language of their birth. On a table by the window were drawing things and paints. On the wall opposite the bed was a painting of a girl in a red dress, with long dark hair, sleeping next to a polar bear.

"This is your room," they said, and now her tears flowed.

The wardrobe was full of clothes for her. The few things she had left behind when she went with the bear were here. They had not known if they would ever see her again, but they had made this room for her, hoping that, one day, she would come back.

The bear had brought her back to her family on Christmas Eve. Downstairs there was a tree, decorated with tiny animals in glowing colours, stitched from felt, twinkling with sequins. Hearts were dotted through the green. Beneath the tree there were presents for all of them, and for her also.

She thanked the bear with all her heart that he had let her come for this day.

During the night a fresh fall of fine snow covered even the bear's footprints, and in the morning they woke to the bright light of sunshine reflecting off a crisp crust of diamond white.

She had brought one special thing with her from her home with the bear, and this she now wrapped in tissue paper and ribbon and placed beneath the tree while everyone was busy in the kitchen.

The joy of being together again, safe and warm, was the best Christmas present that year. At times she would sit back and watch them all, and see her mother slip her hand gently into her father's hand and smile, leaning against his shoulder. They looked young again, and in love.

Christmas dinner was a grand affair. They had been invited to the great house and she was introduced to their benefactor, an old bird of a woman. Her hands were twisted with age and she walked with the help of a stick, but her eyes were bright and dark. The old woman was delighted to meet her, and told her how much she admired her father, his courage and his talent. And so the girl loved her from the start. And she told her how much she enjoyed having the family to stay and how they brought her house back to life.

After they had eaten the old woman gave them each a small present. The girl opened hers, and was astonished to find a necklace of silver and turquoise beads with a bear in the centre, carved from white bone. She darted a look at the old woman, who smiled and nodded to her, a knowing smile. She unclasped the necklace and put it on, and the bone bear drew warmth from her skin.

All afternoon they walked around the grounds of the old house, had snowball fights in the paddocks, stroked the horses in the stables, made huge snowmen. In the evening they opened their presents from under the tree, until there was just one left.

"There is no label on this," her brother said. "Who is it for?"

"For all of you," she answered. "It is a present from me. And from the bear."

There was a hush as she brought the memory of him back into the house. They opened the gift together. It was the photograph of them all, mother, father and all the children, from the time before their troubles. They each looked at it in wonder and passed it on.

Father held it for the longest time, looking back into the past. "How did you get this?" His voice cracked a little as he spoke.

She told him of the silver bell and the morning she had spent thinking of the book of photographs. "I don't think it is a real photograph," she said. "I think those are lost for ever. I think the bear made it for me somehow, from my memory of all the photographs."

Her father thought of his child, miles away from home, in the castle of the bear, remembering her family. "However it came to be, it is beautiful. Thank you, my daughter." He held her close and kissed the top of her head.

It was late when they went off to bed, full to the brim with the happiness of the day. She changed into a long white nightdress and stood for a while looking at the painting of the girl and the bear, twisted trees framing them, a bed of autumn leaves beneath. In the painting the girl slept peacefully. The bear had one eye open.

She still wore the necklace the old woman had given her. She felt the bone bear lying warm on her skin and thought of her bear, all alone on this day. She missed him.

Outside her room she heard the creak of a floorboard.

Her mother knocked gently on the door. "May I come in?" She stood beside her daughter and put her arm round her.

"Where did you get the painting of the bear?"

"It was here when we came. Father wanted to take it down at first. It broke his heart to see it. But the others wouldn't hear of it. It gave them some comfort to see how the bear seemed to be guarding you. So we made this your room. Soon, if ever your father was missing for long, we knew we would find him here. Sometimes he would just be staring at the picture, and sometimes he would come here to write."

"It is very beautiful," the girl said. "Peaceful."

"Do you have to go back? You know that it will break your father's heart again to see you go."

"I do. But you should know that I am happy there. The bear is kind. He needs me somehow. But there is something I don't understand, something I feel I am missing."

They sat down on the bed and her mother took her hand. "Tell me," she said. "Tell me about your journey, about the bear."

And so the girl sat on the bed as the stars shone down to reflect in the snow outside, and on the horizon the Northern Lights danced, unnoticed by all but a fox in the paddock and a cold owl in a hollow oak. She told her mother all that had come to pass, the journey, the castle lair, the beautiful rooms and the books and the bear and the silver bell.

Lulled by tiredness and the warmth of the day she forgot the bear's warning and told her mother of the night-time visitor, and how she could never strike a light to see who or what it was that lay beside her, or reach out to touch, or ask the bear.

When she had finished she climbed into bed, and her mother pulled up the covers round her and kissed her softly. Already asleep when her head touched the pillow, she looked so young. Her mother gently stroked back the hair from her daughter's face and stood for a while, watching as she slept. Then she walked away, and quietly pulled the door shut with a click behind her. She leant back against the door, closed her eyes and sighed, and thought.

The rest of the month went by so fast. The snow melted and the first green spears of snowdrops pushed up through the frosted ground in the avenue.

They spent quiet days sitting by the fire, reading. She found herself listening to music and thinking that the bear would like it, or whilst reading, thought, 'I will take this back with me, we could read this together.' Something would happen during the day and she would think,

'I must tell him about this.' Over and over she told her brothers and sisters about the bear and his enchanted home. She missed him. She would stand in her room and look at the picture, or found herself stroking the bone bear of her necklace. Did the old woman know, she wondered? Or was it just a coincidence?

At night she looked out of her window as the winter landscape began to give way to the first murmur of spring. She watched the path of the moon as it moved across the sky, as it filled and waned to a sliver of silver again, and she looked at the constellation of the Great Bear. She climbed into her bed with its white linen sheets and dreamed of being wrapped in his magnificent whiteness.

As a child she had loved the story of Beauty and the Beast. She had wept when Beauty had forgotten to go back to the Beast, caught up in her life with her family, so that the Beast almost died of loneliness before she remembered him. She wondered how the bear fared without her, and found herself breathless, with a rising sense of panic.

Maybe he would forget her. Maybe he would think

she was so happy with her family that he should leave her there. Maybe he would not come back for her.

A month and a day after Christmas Eve she woke early and ran to the window. The sun was low in the sky. Sharp shadows danced in the snowdrops, deep purples. A blackbird sang. No bear.

All day she waited. When evening came and the family gathered for supper in the kitchen, she was distracted and jumpy. She ate little. Every noise made her rise and go to the window.

Just when they were all preparing to go to bed she heard the sound she had waited for, the sharp knock of a claw against the wood of the door. They all sat and looked from one to the other. No one moved.

Then she stood up and half-walked, half-ran to the door and opened it wide to the winter night. She felt a blush rise to her cheeks. Shyly she greeted the bear and invited him in.

Her heart had lifted at the sight of him. He had

come back for her. She felt shy and awkward and her head swam with swirling emotions.

And so she said a quick goodbye to her family, hugging them close. As she held her mother she felt her push something into her hand, then her mother touched her finger to her lips. Shush. A secret. She kissed her, and then her father, who wept silently to see his daughter taken from him again.

All the while the bear stood and waited.

She picked up the bundle she had hidden behind a cupboard in the kitchen, ready in case he should come, put her mother's gift safe in a pocket, and then she and the bear left the house.

Side by side they walked down the avenue of trees, branches making lace patterns against a sky filled to the brim with stars, and the Milky Way a path of light through it all. Around them the moon-shadows dappled the ground. Her family watched from the door, then, one by one, went back into the warmth of the house – until only her mother remained, leaning on the frame of the door, her finger still touching her lips.

"You do not have to come with me."
They were the first words he said to her as they walked along.

In the moonlight the snowdrops were tiny white stars beneath the trees. Across the paddock a fox screamed.

"I think I know that," she answered. She felt older, walking away from her family.

After a while she reached out a hand and rested it gently on the bear's side. She felt him shudder at her touch.

Looking away from him and up to the sickle moon she said, "I missed you." They walked on a little, side by side, step for step, before she spoke again. "I feared you might forget me."

He stopped, turned to face her. She lifted her hand and he rested his great head against it. "I could wait a thousand years and not forget you. I would travel to the ends of the earth to find you."

His words touched her heart as she held the bear close to her, and then he knelt and she climbed on to his back. Over her shoulder she saw the bright lights of her family's new home, curtains pulled back so they could watch until she was gone from view, light flooding out and spilling over the ground. Ahead, the avenue, a river of darkness.

Then the bear set off at a gallop with the girl holding tight, hands wrapped deep in his thick, warm pelt.

It was early morning when they arrived at the stone door of the bear's enchanted home. The sun had risen, low in the sky, and shone through the trees, making bars of shadow on the ground. Birds filled the air with song.

They spent the day together. She showed him the books she had brought back to read with him, and told him of all she had done.

When she asked him how all had been with him he shook his great head and turned away. "And did you remember what I had said? Not to be alone with your mother? Did she try to get you alone? Did she try to advise you?"

She hesitated a moment and then, "No," she said. "She gave me no advice. We were never alone." With the saying of the words she believed them to be true, even while the weight of her mother's gift hung heavy in her pocket.

He grunted and sighed.

For the rest of the day, from time to time, she would put her hand in her pocket and feel the small box. At last, when it was time to go to bed and she was alone, she took the box out to see what it was, what was inside.

It was small, red and gold, patterned with tiny pieces of mirror glass and beads. Inside, the stub of a candle and another box with three matches.

As she lay down to sleep in her huge curtained bed she tucked her mother's gift under her pillow and began to drift towards a sea of dreams.

Just as she was sinking into sleep she heard the click of the latch. Footsteps moved around the bed. Someone, something, climbed in and settled, with a heartfelt sigh, to sleep.

She waited until whoever or whatever it was had

settled into the rhythmic breathing of deep sleep, then reached her hand under the pillow for the box.

Her own breathing was shallow with excitement. Her heart hammered so loud in her ears she feared it would wake the whole world, as she took out the candle stub and the matches.

Slowly, slowly, she sat up in the bed and leaned towards where the creature was lying. She took out a match. Fingers fumbled to hold the candle, match and box. It was dark, so very dark. The darkness felt like velvet, deep and soft over her eyes. Somewhere in the back of her mind she heard a warning calling, calling, against what she was about to do.

Then she struck the match against the box. A flower of orange flame blossomed so bright and a petal caught to the candle wick. Light flooded out and filled every corner of the room. She blinked in its brightness and then saw, lying beside her, the most beautiful young man she had ever seen. His dark hair sprayed out over the pillow, his skin pale, almost white, alabaster. A moment of watching as he slept so peacefully, then she leaned towards him.

Three drops of hot wax dripped from the candle in her hand and fell on to his white, white shirt. His eyes opened and she saw that they were the dark, sad eyes of the bear, deep pools of sorrow. For the briefest moment he looked at her face in the warm candlelight and she knew that she loved him, had always loved him and would always love him, to the end of time and the ends of the earth.

Then he lifted his hands to his face and cried out and his cry was wild, deep and full of despair.

The hot wax burned her fingers. Terrified by his wildness, she fumbled to light the lantern, and as more light filled the room she began to shake.

"What have I done? What have I done? Did I burn you, are you in pain?" Fear gripped her heart and her words came out as sobs.

It was only this that brought him back to calm. He reached across the bed and took her in his arms, and held her and rocked her until her sobbing ceased.

For a while they stayed like this, until all was quiet. Her mother's candle had long since guttered out, leaving a bitter smell of smoke in the air. She wiped away the last of her tears on the sleeve of her nightdress and pulled away, the better to see his face, but he turned away from her.

She reached out a hand, and turned his face towards her until she saw again his beautiful, dark, wild eyes. "What have I done?" she asked. She traced her fingers over his lips, through his hair and he reached his hand towards her, but then shook his head and pulled away. "Tell me," she said. "What have I done?"

"You have broken the enchantment." His voice was heavy with sadness. But why? She did not understand. He said that she had broken the enchantment. In stories this was the moment Snow White came alive again, where Sleeping Beauty woke to live happy ever after with her Prince. Somehow she had broken the enchantment and now all would be well.

She tried to smile, but he just shook his head.

Here beside her in the bed was the most beautiful man she had ever seen, and with all her heart she knew that she loved him. But all was not well.

He reached across and took her hand, held it briefly to his lips and kissed it. Her heart flew like a bird inside her, battering its wings. "So sorry. It is all my fault. I should not have let you go to them. I should have kept you here. I should not have come to you every night, but I so longed to be near you. I waited so long to find you. I lived through so much loneliness. And you are so beautiful. I thought no harm would come. Just to be close to you."

They lay down together in the bed and he wrapped her in his arms and held her. He smelled of wildness and of frost. His raven hair still held the musky smell of bear. She began to understand.

By candlelight they lay and he told her what she already knew in her heart.

"Almost one thousand years ago I was a prince, without worries or cares. Out hunting one day, a troll queen saw me and took me away as a pet for her child, a plaything. As I grew, the daughter fell in love with me and when I refused her the mother put an enchantment on me. I would live for a thousand years as a bear, unless I

61

could find someone who would love me. She had to live with me for a year and a day. She had to come with me and stay with me of her own free will. At night the enchantment would break and I could walk again as a man, but by day I would always become a bear. And she must never see me as anything other than a bear.

"I found you. I couldn't believe it when I found you. You called to me across continents, across night and day, across time. Through your dreams, your heart sang to me."

She turned her face to his and they kissed. Just once.

"In three days' time it would have been a year and a day. If I had been patient, if I had stayed away, you would not have seen me and we would be free. But I was drawn to you as a moth to a flame. I could not stay away. All the candles in the room were enchanted so they could not light, so that you could not see me. I thought I was safe. But you brought the candle from home, the matches your mother gave you. Now all is lost and it is all my fault."

"And if I had listened to you, not used the candle...

but you came every night and I wondered who or what you were. My mother gave me no advice, just the means to see in the dark. I should have waited. I should have listened to you. What will happen? Can we run away together now? We could go to my family – all will be...."

He put his fingers to her lips and shook his head. "Now I must go to the Troll Queen's daughter, to be her husband. She lives in the castle that lies East of the Sun and West of the Moon. I have this one night left and then I must go."

"No." She shook her head. "No, you cannot, I will not let you." She loved him. She loved him as the bear, she loved him as the man. She would not let him go.

He held her close. "I'm sorry, so sorry. So long I have waited. If I could stay I would."

"But where is this castle? East of the Sun and West of the Moon? Where is that? I will come with you."

"No, you cannot."

"Then I will find you. This time I will be the one to search until I find you, to the end of time, to the ends of the earth. I will search until I find you and we will be together. I love you."

All night they talked. They lay together side by side until weariness overcame them both and they slept, her head pillowed on his shoulder, her hand resting on his heart.

The sun woke her, shining through the leaves, warm on her face. For a few seconds she lay still, while the light played and danced across her closed eyes. She could smell the earth, and the breeze played with her hair. Birds sang. The wind moved in the leaves of the trees like music.

She opened her eyes and sat up slowly, looking around. He was gone.

The bed was gone, the room, the enchanted palace, everything. Gone.

She was alone in a forest clearing, sleeping on a small conical mound of grass and flowers, and he was gone.

Beside her lay the bundle of things that she had brought with her when she first left her family to live with the bear. Her hand moved to her neck. She still wore the turquoise and silver necklace, and the bone bear was warm against her skin. She knew now that she had loved him when he was a bear, even before she saw him as a man.

At the edge of the clearing she saw a twitch of movement, two brown eyes, and hope rose in her heart. But it was only a deer, watching from the dappled shade.

He was gone. Despair settled over her like a heavy blanket and she crumpled to the ground, her body wracked with sobs.

He was gone to the castle that lay East of the Sun and West of the Moon and she was more alone than she had ever been in her life.

How long she lay in the forest clearing she could not say. Long enough for the forest animals to come close, for deer to crop the grass and flowers around her, for a robin to rest on her shoulder. Long enough for ravens to gather in the ring of trees around her, thinking she was carrion.

At last she exhausted herself with weeping, slept, then woke again. It was dusk now. Long shadows and a glimpse of the moon through silvered leaves. Around her the forest rustled with evening sounds. Birds sang and here and there a woodpigeon called a song that spoke to her alone. "He is gone, far away; he is gone, far away." Night washed the colour from everything and the primroses that decorated her forest bed shone white on the ground. All around owls hooted.

She was hungry. She was cold and lost and hungry. Sorrow wrapped itself around her heart like a cold fist.

She gathered up her bundle and began to walk. She did not know which way to go, but instinct led her up, above the trees, to get her bearings. She moved through the forest slowly, a black-and-white forest where the wind whispered lullabies in the leaves, while her feet cracked twigs like dry and broken bones.

Up and up, all through the night, and never a sign of a lamp or a light. Then out on to a clear hill high above the forest canopy, and the sky a dizzying swirl of stars.

She stood on the hill in the clearing. The moon painted the forest all around and she could see where it silvered a pathway across the sea. Clouds strung a necklace around the horizon, dark, making holes in the starry sky. A shooting star drew a glorious trail through the night. The more she looked up the more stars she could see, stretching away into infinite space. She felt small, so small. She was alone for the first time in her life. She was lost. The bear was gone. Her love was taken to a place, she knew not where, only that it lay East of the Sun, West of the Moon.

She looked towards the moon, and then at the last vestige of light clinging to the sky where the sun had set. And she tried to find the place in the world that lay East of the Sun and West of the Moon.

As the first light of day began to paint colour back into the world, she gathered herself in from where her thoughts had spread. Alone, yes, but she knew that he loved her too. He had waited for her, watched for her, for a thousand years. She would search for him now, and find him even if it took a lifetime. They would be together. Knowing that he loved her eased her loneliness a little.

As the tip of the moon dropped into the ocean on the horizon, she set off to find her love, in the castle that lay East of the Sun and West of the Moon.

She walked. By day and by night she walked, resting when she was tired. She had no money and no food, only the clothes she wore and the few things in her small bundle. On the first day she found the silver bell inside the bundle, and her hopes rose. She shook the bell, wishing only for a loaf of bread and a flask of water. Nothing. The enchantment had been broken and the bell no longer worked. At the next town she took it into an antique shop and traded it for a long warm velvet coat, red, with a fur-lined hood and long sleeves.

She walked, day after day, night after night. She walked in the mornings when spiders' webs, heavy with dew, silvered the path before her. She walked in the middle of the day when the heat of the air washed over her skin, wrapping her in warmth. She walked in the evenings when the low sun made deep shadows and painted everything with gold and red. She walked at night when the stars or the moon lit her path.

Only when she was walking could her mind be steady, and she walked as if to walk away the madness of loss that clung to her. She walked through rain and fog and sun and snow.

Some days she would marvel at the beauty of the world around her, the play of light over a landscape of fields, the wind in corn, rippling the grass like water, the wind stroking her face, scented with heather, honeysuckle.

Some days she walked trapped inside her head, turning over her memories of the bear, trying to fix in her mind's eye the face of her love and his sad, dark eyes. These days held an edge of madness. If she was lucky she would be startled out of herself by the brilliant flash of a kingfisher or the scream of hawks overhead. Otherwise she would sink into despair.

When she was tired she rested and dreamed of walking, or sleeping, as the girl in the painting in her bedroom at home had slept, wrapped in the huge bear's paws.

She ate wild strawberries, blackberries and cherries, hawthorn leaves, sweet chestnuts baked in a fire, mushrooms flavoured with wild thyme, apples and pears and peaches and pomegranates, wild carrot and hedge garlic, elder flowers and elder berries, almonds, peaches and apricots, wild raspberries, cloudberries and bilberries.

One evening she startled a fox as it was taking a pheasant to its cubs. It dropped the bird and ran, and that night she wrapped the bird in leaves and baked it in the embers of the fire. She learned to tickle for trout and salmon in clear mountain streams where trees shaded the water.

One evening she came upon fields, humped with

pillowed rows of purple flowers, heaven-scented. A lavender farm. The scent took her back to her scented baths in the bear's enchanted palace and she lay down to rest for a while between the rows of flowers. Lulled by the gentle drone of the bees and the sweet scent that built in the air as the sun set, she slept.

In the morning a child sat by her side, the farmer's daughter. She thought the sleeping woman in the field must be a fairy princess, her long hair trailed through with lavender flowers. The farmer's daughter took her home and gave her breakfast and when she went on her way, a small bouquet of lavender to keep in her pocket.

Sometimes she would meet people along the path and stop to talk a while, ask if they knew of the castle. But no one did. Sometimes people would share their food with her, or she would shelter in a barn and work a little in exchange for food. But she would never stay for more than a day. She had to keep moving on.

She walked through the spring, and the smell of the earth breaking as new shoots pushed through was strong. The wild March wind ran its fingers through her long hair, winding it into tangled tresses.

She walked in the summer when the heat of the air drew the perfume from flowers and kept it safe until evening. Warm winds washed her face.

She walked in the autumn when leaves swirled around her and fruits hung heavy on bowing branches. Through rain and sun and snow she walked, through winter, when her feet crunched the crust of white snow, and the north wind kissed her awake on freezing mornings.

At first the forest animals fled from her, but as she walked day after day it was as if they recognised her as one of their own, a wild thing. She could walk through a herd of deer and they would barely raise their heads to watch her pass.

For the most part she avoided cities, only going into them when hunger became too much, less and less often as time went on and she learned where to find food, and how to live with the lack of it. She was becoming a wild thing.

But there came a day when she was tired and hungry, cold and wet. The low mist had pushed her thoughts inside her head and she felt that no matter how far she walked she would never reach the castle, never see her love again and that all was lost. She knew that tomorrow, if she did not find food she would have to take her last precious thing to town to sell. Her fingers played with the bone bear on her turquoise necklace and it felt warm in her hand. Tomorrow.

W hen she woke in the morning she felt dazed with hunger. Something warm was licking her face. Half awake, half asleep, she thought that it was her bear. She opened her eyes and stretched out to wrap her arms around him and lose herself in his whiteness. Not her bear. She saw the small black nose and bright brown eyes of a black dog.

"Come away now, and leave her in peace." The voice of a woman.

"I thought you would never wake. Now, let's get you home."

It was a woman, tall beside her, towering, with long black hair, long skirt down to the floor, and boots. She leaned on a stick. Behind her a horse cropped the grass and nosed among the flowers. All drifted in and out of focus. The girl tried to speak but the words fell about in her mouth. She tried to rise, stumbled and sank into darkness.

"She's awake. She's awake".

The voice came from a bird, black as coal with bright blue button eyes. He sat on the mantle over the fire and bobbed his head. "She's awake, awake."

At the fire a woman turned. "Indeed she is. And how are you feeling?"

It took the girl a while to gather herself up. It seemed as if she had floated away into a sea of darkness, a sea full of dreams. Slowly she brought herself back.

The room was small. A fire burned in the hearth, the wood crackling and hissing out sap, green flame dancing like witch-fire. A smell of food brought back the sharp pains of hunger. She was warm, rested.

"Where am I? Who are you? So hungry." Her hand shot to her neck, but she felt at once the warm weight of her necklace.

"Don't worry, my dear. The bird likes shiny pretty things, but we are not thieves and your necklace is safe. I recognised you by it, though I would have known you anywhere. And not many young girls come wandering so very far from home, alone in the woods, and faint away at my feet. Never mind your questions for a while. I will answer what I can, and what I can't will have to wait. Now, you have walked a long way and you have longer yet to travel. Rest here and let us build up your strength."

She handed the girl a small bowl, steaming with soup, and a carved wooden spoon.

As she ate, the girl looked around. The woman was not old. Maybe the same age as her mother. She had long black hair and blue eyes as bright as the bird's. A kind face, soft. The room was filled with things. Herbs hung, drying in bunches from the ceiling. Boxes, jars, bottles and books filled the shelves around the wall.

"Thank you." She handed back an empty bowl and the woman passed her a cup of herb tea sweetened with honey.

"Now, tell me what it is you seek."

For a moment the girl just looked at her. It was many months since she had talked other than to answer a greeting from a passing stranger. "I seek," she said, "the castle that lies East of the Sun and West of the Moon." It was so simple, but when she spoke the words aloud it suddenly seemed so strange.

"Yes. I knew it was you. Could be no other. So, you are the one that should have had him. You are the one he waited for all those years and now he waits again. I hoped it was you when I found you in the woods, and wearing the necklace and all."

"So you know him." Relief flooded her voice. It had sounded so strange spoken aloud again. East of the Sun and West of the Moon, a fairy tale. But this woman knew him. "You know him, you know where he is. I must go to him, now, I must go. Help me."

"Steady now, steady." The woman sat down on the bed and put her hand on the girl's shoulder. "I said

I know of him. I know of the castle. But where it lies is a mystery to most and few have ever found it. You still have a long way to go. I do not know where it is but I can help you. First you must rest and gather your strength. Eat, sleep and be warm. And no more walking for you, you have walked far enough. You must go to my sister who lives a long way from here. I have a horse I will lend you. My sister is older and wiser than me. She may know where the castle is."

The girl's head was full of questions. How did the woman know of the castle, of her story and of her love? It seemed that she had waited for her here at the end of her road. She feared that if she had not found the woman, or been found by her she would have died of hopelessness and hunger.

"Sleep now. Sleep now." From the mantle the black bird chirred its words as if they were a spell for sleeping. She felt her eyes grow heavy, peace filled her mind and she fell into a dreamless sleep.

Over the next few days she ate and slept, helped the woman with simple tasks and teased the black bird with ears of corn. Together they sat on the doorstep, shelling green peas in the evening sunshine. They walked a little through the woods around the house and the woman showed her more plants, what to eat and what to avoid. She showed her how to hook a bright red hawthorn berry to a thread and tempt a fish to taste it. Conversation was slight and sparse, as between two people at ease in their own company after long periods of solitude.

She showed her how to take honey from the hives she kept in a small, wild orchard of apple trees, without disturbing the bees. And the girl sat on the rise behind the house and watched the sun move across the sky, the wind build castles of clouds in the blue. It felt good to be in one place, to be still.

For a few days she almost forgot about her task. It was so pleasant to wake up in the same bed day after day, until the seventh morning, when she woke to the bird saying, "Go now, go now."

The woman packed into her bundle bread and cherries,

apples and goat's cheese, a flask of mead and a bottle of water, and a jar of golden honey with honeycomb.

"It is time to leave now, dear. But go with my blessing, and my horse. He knows the way, as he knows many things. When you get to my sister's house just tweak his left ear, gently, mind, and whisper 'Home now, go home', and he will come back to me."

Outside, the horse waited, a stocky mountain beast with a wind-twisted mane. No saddle or bridle. The girl climbed clumsily on to his back and a memory of riding the bear slipped into her mind, unbidden.

"I have a gift for you." The woman's voice pushed aside her reverie.

"Oh, but I have nothing to give you, and you have been so good to me, so very kind."

The woman smiled. She took the girl's hands in hers and looked carefully at her palm. She frowned. Then into her hand dropped an apple.

Small and perfect, the skin had the waxy quality of an apple, and it smelled like an apple picked fresh from a tree in early autumn. But the colour was of gold, and by the weight of it she knew it to be of the purest gold.

As it fell into her hand she felt the mysterious tingle of magic run through her blood.

"Keep it safe and keep it hidden. There are those on the road who would want to take it from you. And your necklace too. The world can be a wicked place. Not all those you meet will want to help you. You will know when the time is right how and when to use the apple. Now go. Be brave, be clever and be true to your heart. And give my love to my sister."

She put the apple safe inside her bundle, wrapped in a velvet scarf. She tucked her necklace safe under her clothes, stooped down from the height of the horse's back and kissed the top of her friend's head. Then she turned the horse's head, kicked gently with her heels and they set off, walking steadily up the hill.

By the door of the house the woman watched for a while, and from the roof the black bird called, "Go well, go well."

Then she turned and sighed and went inside.

On the back of the horse the girl daydreamed that she was riding her white bear across the starry sky.

The horse was quiet and knew the way, and it was pleasant to be moving again. It had been good to rest, and the woman had been the best sort of company. But now at last she felt that each step was taking her closer to her love.

Somehow, seeking the woman's sister seemed more achievable than finding the castle that lay East of the Sun and West of the Moon. She had hope again.

The days were long, but the journey was pleasant, through silver-birch forests where golden leaves of autumn played a beautiful tune with the breeze, and the light painted dappled gold pennies on the rich earth beneath the horse's hooves.

They travelled down mountain slopes where sheep nibbled the pasture to look like velvet. She saw lynx in the mountains, secret, cold-eyed cats. Red foxes watched as they passed, and a brown bear, fat and ready for hibernation, looked up from harvesting a berry bush. He too watched as they passed, then went back to his feast. Once the horse was spooked by the shadow of wolves moving through the trees on a parallel pathway.

Each night they rested and she picked handfuls of sweet grass flavoured with late autumn flowers and fed them to the horse. She fell asleep to the sound of the animal's regular pull and crunch as it grazed close by.

In the mornings they would find a stream and drink, and she would jump on to the horse's back. She loved the sweet, warm smell of him, a smell like summer, that clung to her hands and to her clothes. Each day she woke to sunshine. Each evening a breath of autumn edged in. Their days fell into a pattern.

So she was surprised when the horse stopped in a clearing, within a wood. All around, twisted oaks lay close to the ground, ancient and ringed with mountain ash, berries bright in the sunlight. Off the path the ground was uneven, with rocks covered in deep cushions of thick, soft moss, greener than emeralds. The wood was quiet, but for the faintest rustle of falling leaves.

She could almost hear the wings of the woodland brown butterflies as they lifted, circling upwards in a dance with the leaves.

She kicked the horse gently, but he snorted and stood, stamping. He would not go on. The hair on the back of her neck prickled. She slid down from the horse's high back on to the mossy ground.

At the edge of the clearing the ground sloped up to a wall of rock, and only as she walked closer did she see that it was not a slope, but a roof, covered with turf and late flowering honeysuckle.

On the roof was a black bird, with a dagger of a beak. He bobbed and bowed and jumped closer, his feathers purple in the sunlight. Strange chortling, whirring sounds came from him. Then he screamed a loud *Cark* and fixed her with his cold, round eye. Looking her over, he declared, "She's here. She's here."

"And not before time too." Behind her stood a woman, long grey hair reaching down her back in a plait. Older than her sister, but alike in other ways. "You took your time getting here. I would say by the look of you that your journey was pleasant?"

The big black bird flew down and landed on the girl's shoulder, making her jump. He pulled at her hair with his beak.

"And you can leave her alone, Trouble. Come along in, dear. Pleasant journey or not, you must be tired. Come. I have some supper ready for you."

The rook hopped from the girl's shoulder to the back of the horse as the girl found her manners. "I bring you greetings from your sister. She sent me to you. Your sister said that you might know, might be able to tell me the way I need to go to find the castle...."

"East of the Sun and West of the Moon. Yes, yes, well, no. I know of it, who lives there. How they came there, and of your prince that you should have had. But the way there or where it is – that's a mystery beyond my reckoning."

The girl felt hope slipping away.

"But I know someone who can help you, and that is the next best thing. So don't look so lost and forlorn. It doesn't suit you. Let's get my sister's old nag back on his way, then come inside and we'll see what we can do."

She showed the girl where she kept her hay and they gave the horse a handful or two. She brushed him down, thanked him for his help and then twisted his left ear gently round her fingers and whispered, "Home now, go home." And then, "Safe journey, gentle beast." And with a flick of his tail he trotted off.

For seven days she rested. She sat in the sun outside the house while bees buzzed in the last of the flowers on the roof, and the rook chortled and croaked an endless stream of mutterings, hopping about with mischief in his eye.

The woman kept sheep and she spent much of her time carding and combing the wool, pulling out tangles and goose-grass and burs. She taught the girl how to straighten and soften the wool ready for spinning. And one evening as they sat together she began to run a comb through the girl's wind-tangled hair. It reminded her so much of her mother brushing and combing her hair when she was a child that she felt the enormous distance of space and time open between them. Soft tears fell silently.

Days and evenings were companionable, but again on the seventh a restlessness returned and blew up like the wind.

"It is time you were off, my dear. If you still want to find him?"

"That is what I wish for more than anything," said the girl.

"Be careful what you wish for. Seldom, when our wishes come true, do we find that we have what we truly desired. Wishes have ways of twisting themselves, turning unexpected corners."

The girl frowned. She had thought of little other than finding her love since waking without him all those months, or was it years ago. She had started on this path, without question stayed on it. Had it become habit?

The woman whistled, long and low. Moments later a horse, dark as a moonless night, trotted out from between the trees.

"You may take the horse. He knows where to go.

Just stay on him and feed him well. He will take you to my sister's house. If anyone knows where your true love lies it will be her. She loved once, but lost him, for he was wild. When you get to her house twist the horse's left ear, say 'Home now, home, sweet horse' and he will find his way back to me. And take this with you. You will know, when the time comes, how and when to use it." She handed the girl a carding comb, very plain but beautifully crafted and made from rich red gold. It was heavy and warm in her hand.

A golden apple, a carding comb. Somehow they would help her, and somehow having them gave her confidence that however long it took, she would reach her goal.

"Thank you, it is beautiful. It will remind me of you."

"Off with you now, girl, you are wasting daylight." And the woman gave her horse one last pat.

As they disappeared together back into the forest, the rook flew to the old woman's shoulder.

"A long road ahead, ahead," said the rook.

"And a test or two to face, my dear," she said and stroked the rook on his head.

91

Out through the forest and into mountain valleys, by streams that pooled under waterfalls hung with green ferns. At night the girl slept to a chorus of frogs sawing their songs. Herons flew up, heavy-winged birds, from the banks of streams, and dippers bobbed under the water and hopped along rocks. Wagtails, yellow and grey, danced on the road before her.

The horse was steady, no saddle or bridle. She held his mane wrapped around her hand. He was sure of the way.

After many days they came to the edge of a desert where a tent stood in the shelter of tall trees. Through all of the trees wind chimes hung, made of wood and metal and bone, and on top of the tallest tree perched the biggest, blackest bird she had ever seen, beak like a dagger and dark, round eyes.

"Come and see. Come and see." His voice rang like a deep bell across the desert.

Out of the tent came a figure dressed from head to foot in black. The person was old, she could tell, but had an elegance she had never seen before in anyone. Only her eyes were visible, and by these alone the girl could tell she had come to the right place.

"Inside, inside," the bird called down.

The old woman busied herself, taking in the wind chimes which had begun to clang and clamour. She turned to see the girl and the horse. "At last." This barely heard against the rising of the wind. "Come in, come in, we need to get you both inside, or the wind and the sand will fill your lungs and that will be an end to it all."

Around them the black bird hopped and pulled at the chimes, whistling and crying, "Quick, quick, hurry hurry."

As she followed the old woman into the tent, the hot wind of the desert stroked her cheek like a kiss, and she turned to see, far out on the horizon, the sand moving like water, wave after wave rolling towards them, sand made liquid by the force of the wind.

The woman pulled her inside, away from the storm.

A few moments more and the pressure from the wind would have sucked the air from her and filled her lungs with the burning grains of sand.

Inside the tent the air was still. The horse wandered into a corner where a beautiful white horse was already calmly crunching at a bag of sweet hay, hung from the tent roof.

The light inside was dim, tinted blue by the canvas. The walls were lined with beautiful carpets of rich colours. Birds and animals, flowers and fruit, winged lions and dragons danced in incredible designs, woven into the rugs.

The woman shook off her black veil and the girl saw her face for the first time. Old, yes, but beautiful too, skin bronzed by the weather, lined by the passing of time, wise. This was perhaps the most beautiful woman she had ever seen. The woman's face was marked by life, by knowledge, by experience. Her bearing was one of confidence. She knew her place in the world and was at peace with herself. Never before had the girl really looked at an old person.

For a while the woman busied herself untangling

the wind chimes and hanging them in a corner of the tent, where they still rang as the storm outside shook and buffeted the walls. "You were lucky to come when you did. Storms in the desert can be dangerous things and I think this one was sent for you."

The woman went to a chest and took out four stones, smooth rectangles with deep grooves marked all round them, ochre-coloured. She stood them in the four corners of the tent and whispered an incantation. The walls of the tent stilled, and the wind chimes hushed.

"How did you do that?" the girl asked. The woman fascinated her.

"A poet once said,

The wind in one's face
makes one wise

and I have known the wind for many years. Most things come through learning, and you will have to learn fast if you are to reach your goal and keep your life. And the wind stones help, of course." The woman smiled. "But before learning more, you should eat."

They shared flat bread and dates, grapes and goat's cheese, and drank the sweetest water drawn from the woman's well before the sandstorm blew in.

"How did you know I was coming? And how did you know the storm would come?"

"You learn many things with age, girl. The first being that the more you know the more you see you have yet to learn. Your coming was easy, for birds fly and birds talk. The raven watched your journey. And the storm came to greet you. You have travelled far, but the hardest part of a journey is always the next step. You are brave and strong. You will need to be, for now you must seek the help of the wind.

"I know many things. I know of your love for the one who waits, East of the Sun, West of the Moon. I know that time is running short. The storm was sent as a greeting to you by the one whose help you will need. A greeting or a warning. I will teach you what I can in the short time that we have. It may help."

All the while the girl ate and watched the woman as she spoke, her voice like a prayer or a spell.

"The wind is a strange creature, four and one at the same time. He can purr like a cat one minute, then roar like a tiger. At one time you can feel him like a kiss on your cheek, the next he will push you to the ground and steal your breath away." She spoke with a faraway look in her eyes and her words were those of a wise lover who knows well the moods of her love.

"He has no physical form, can take whatever shape is dearest to your heart. He is everywhere and nowhere. He plays with our lives like a cat with a mouse, at times benevolent, spreading seeds and blowing fair to speed a ship on its way. At others the same wind that spread the seeds of life will carry disease and death. Boats will rock in the arms of a storm or lie with never a whisper to fill their sails, as all on board thirst as much for wind as for water.

"He is a trickster, a charmer. He will steal away your heart. Because he has no heart of his own."

And now her voice dropped to a whisper, almost to nothing, mixing with the music of the gale outside, and a heavy tear filled each eye. "I know, because he took mine."

The girl felt a chill fill the blue light of the tent, as if the wind had crept in through a chink or a crack.

Then the woman shook her head as if to shake away

the memor,y and the spell was broken. "Enough. You need rest. If I am right the storm will last a while and there will be time for me to tell you more."

She pointed to a bedroll in the corner and the girl lay down and watched as the woman moved around, clearing the remains of the meal and then settling at a spinning wheel. She spun a fine yarn of deep red wool, and as the wheel spun she sang a song, quiet and low, in harmony with the wind outside and the clack and click of the spinning wheel.

The words of the song were lost to the girl's hearing but all seemed so familiar. She tried to imagine this old woman as she had once been. She too had been in love, with a passion that burned her heart, but she had lost her love. In all her wanderings, the thought that something so strong could be lost to her had never seemed so real. The rhythm of the wind and the song and the wheel turned in her mind until she dreamt of her bear, lost in a desert of white, a crystal tear frozen in each dark eye.

Over the next few days, while the storm raged outside, the woman told the girl all she could of the nature of the world's winds, and while they talked she taught her to spin.

She told her of the wind stones that protected the tent, stones where people thought the soul of the wind was kept. People nearby called her La Baragouin and believed her to be a priestess who could summon winds to order. They came to her with requests to give fair winds to felugas on the river, to speed their trade and help them prosper, to blow away ill-will and storms.

She told her how, in some places, people still believed that to turn away a storm you should meet a wind with knives and swords. How in other places people hung flags, decorated with prayers, which would imprint upon the wind with every moment of its passing, and carry the prayers around the world.

She spoke of the wind witches of old who would sell a fair wind or foul, trapped in a knotted string. "Three knots, one for a breeze, one for a strong wind and the third never to be untied, but it had to be there, to make the spell work."

She told of the people in the far north whose knowledge of and reverence for the wind was such that they could sail a boat wherever they wished, even on the calmest of days.

"Each of the winds has its own character, and yet they are all one, and he has many names. Some call him Fohn, Favonious, Dzhani, Galerna Maestral, Marin or Kusi, and Labech. In Mexico they call the wind Santa Ana, and he brings madness and murder, like the Mistral. In Italy Zephyrus spreads light thistledown to decorate the streets until it blows into corners and lies like snow. Koochee whirls like a demon round the Australian desert. In Brazil Minuano freezes the peasants in their fields. Matsubori steals the secrets of lovers in Japan and throws them around the mountains while Kamakaza, sickle wind, cuts like a knife. The Algonquin call him Kabeyun, the father of winds, while in Morocco Khamsin flies hot and dusty across the face of the earth.

"He will rise from a Cat's Paw wind, enough to put a ripple on a still pool of water, to a Cyclone, with no thought to anyone or anything. Many tales are told of him. The West Wind, Zephyrus, was a cruel and stormy wind. It is said that he fell in love with a nymph, Chloris, beautiful and pale, delicate and kind. His love changed his wild spirit and for Chloris he became a breeze, warm and soft, that carried always the sweet scent of flowers, for her and her alone. But she was mortal and she grew old and died."

La Baragouin seemed to retreat into her thoughts and her hand moved over the skin of her face, beautiful, but old. She sighed and shook her head.

"In dying she became a flower, white and lovely, Ancmone. Now he carries her seeds around the world in his hands and scatters them on mountainsides, in woodlands, wherever they will grow, to cover the land with her image and her sweet perfume. He is neither good nor evil, beyond both. Many names he carries and many moods, but all are one. Do you understand?"

"I try to," said the girl, "but it is difficult to hold in my mind."

"And always remember that he has no heart."

Day after day they sat, and the wind howled outside and the spinning wheels turned, and she learned much, but never enough. It was dark, for the sandstorm fed on what light there was. In the corner the horses stamped and munched, spooked by the wind but lulled by the gentle talk and the spin of the wheels.

As the girl came out of her dreaming on the seventh morning she knew that the storm had ended. Clear birdsong rang out, and a blue light filled the four corners of the tent.

The old woman was already up and had taken the wind stones from the corners, washed them in fresh water and dusted them with a fresh layer of ochre. The tent flap was pegged back and a light breeze blew in cool air, a hint of dew still clinging heavy to it.

Outside, the landscape had been carved into fresh shapes by the wind's hand. The desert extended into the pathway the girl had followed. It was as if the storm had blown the tent high across the sky and set it down in another place – mischievous, confusing.

"It is time to put my sister's horse back on his way. Then we must get you back on your path."

So the girl held the horse's ear and whispered the incantation to send him home, with her thanks.

"Now you must ride again, and my horse will carry you to where the East Wind waits. If you are lucky he will know where your love lies and he will take you there. But I fear that only the North Wind is old enough, wise enough and strong enough to be your guide. Do not trust him."

They readied the horse, handsome and fine, white as her bear and almost as swift as the wind. She leapt lightly on to his back.

"I have gifts also. You know now how to send the horse back when you reach your goal and to trust him to know the way. Take this also. You will know, when the time comes, how to use it."

She handed the girl a small version of the spinning wheel. Small but beautifully crafted, each piece, wheel, axle, footman and treadle, maiden and bobbin, flyer and whorl all made from different-coloured gold. "The bearings are made from gold too and oiled with ambergris. Take it and take care. And this also."

She handed her a crimson cape of finest spun wool. "Only a cape to warm you in the desert at night, but the fastening is a wind-witch spell. Three knots. Remember, one for a light breeze, the second for a strong wind and the third you must never even loosen. If the East and the West and the South cannot help you, you will have to face Him. He will try and trick you, steal your heart. He is beautiful and powerful."

Again the girl saw the bright pearls of tears in the woman's eyes and the years seemed to drop from her face.

"He is beautiful." Almost a whisper. "And he will try to steal your heart. Because he has no heart."

The girl took the cape and wrapped it around her shoulders and caught the witch-spell in her hand. She felt again the warm tingle of magic run through her. "I will try. I will do the best that I can. Thank you."

She turned the horse's head and began to ride across

the endless sea of sand.

As the old woman watched her go she began to hang the chimes back in their places in the trees.

"He will try to steal her heart away," she said to the black raven, who watched also, from the tallest tree. "Do you think she has the strength to succeed?"

The raven barked a deep croak and soared into the air to follow. Against the might and the will and the cold cunning of the great North Wind, the girl was as slight and insignificant as an aspen leaf.

How could she possibly succeed?

Across the desert she rode. She passed settlements with yurts, small camel herds where families stood, shading their eyes, and watched the girl on horseback. Sometimes a child raised a hand in greeting.

Here in this vast open space the modern world intruded as it had not done before. A line of poles stretched across the sand carrying electricity from one side of the desert to the other, leaving a scar across the face of the land. In the huge open sky, aeroplanes drew lines that hung for a while, marking their passage, then blew away in the wind.

At night she fell asleep watching satellites sail around the world, far-off starships. The moon rose, red in the dark sky. The desert took on all colours, ochre, umber, orange, vermillion, then purple with deep ultramarine shadows.

All through the desert the wind teased her, tangling his fingers through her hair and winding it into tresses so that no matter how she tied it, before long it would weave around her head like snakes. He stroked her cheeks, blew cooler air when the heat became too much. He played with her. He drew shapes in the sand with tumbling weed for her. He swept up waves of sand and shaped them to run behind her like wild wind horses, a great herd, keeping pace with her horse. He caught snatches of music and carried them to her ears, at night, gentle lullabies, in the morning, birdsong. He blew a flower over the desert and placed it in her hand.

Gentle as a cat, fierce as a tiger, even as they played she could see where wind and time had cut through the hardest stone, sculpting it into high waves of smooth rock.

She came to a place where, over thousands and thousands of years, the wind had shaped red rocks to perfect spheres, dropped on to a flat plain, for all the world like a giant game of marbles.

She began to fall in love. The desert was beautiful. At night it was cold, the days hot. On waking, the air was filled with a heavy dew. Within minutes it was carried away by the heat of the day.

She thought little. All the while she rode she turned over in her mind the names of the wind, for knowing the name of a thing gives power. She did not feel powerful, but she did feel something drawing her on, closer and closer.

Overhead, vultures circled.

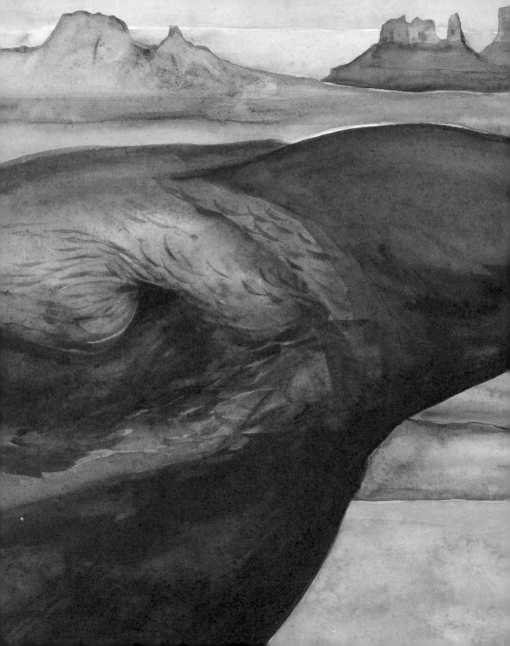

All too soon she came to the home of the East Wind. She sent the horse home to La Baragouin with her thanks, and turned to face him.

"So, you are the one he waits for." The East Wind looked her over and she thought he spoke of her prince in the castle.

"Can you take me to him?"

"I can take you to my brother. He is stronger than I. The castle that lies East of the Sun and West of the Moon is not easily reached. He may be able to help. Are you ready to ride with the wind?"

"I will ride wherever I need to go to be with my love."

"Then come. Time runs away and the one who waits is not known for his patience." And he lifted her into his arms like a child.

She had often dreamed of flying, but now she moved across the face of the earth in the arms of the East Wind. At the head of the wind there was a place of great stillness. She looked down, and below it seemed that the earth turned for her and her alone.

They flew over hills. Mountains, valleys, dropped

away beneath them. They flew over forests, dipping to bend the treetops, across lakes where they wrinkled and rippled the water to waves, and through cornfields that rippled and swayed like water. Higher they blew the great clouds into shapes and built castles and dragons to dance in the air. Together they chased the birds through the sky, and she felt that she had not lived until this day.

The East Wind carried her as gently as he could, and swiftly. His smell was of spices, cinnamon and ginger, paprika and vanilla. Soft on the wind she rode, until they came to the house of the West Wind.

"I can see why he wants you," the West Wind said. "Many would run away, but you move ever towards him, closer and closer. Are you not afraid?"

"I will go to my love, at whatever cost. Do you know the way? Can you take me to the castle, East of the Sun, West of the Moon?"

"Even if I knew how, I could never take you. I fear there is only one with the strength and knowledge for such a journey, but there is a chance you may yet be saved. My brother, the South Wind, is almost as strong and he knows much. Let it be hoped that he can take you."

Again she was lifted, now in the arms of the West Wind, over the sea so low that white crests of water made rainbows dance in the sunlight.

She began to fear. She was so close now. Two more chances.

The South Wind might not know the way and the North Wind could not be trusted. Even as she flew over trees that bent behind them, with the wonder of the world spread beneath her, she felt her heart sinking, slipping into a dark place, where a fear of failure caught her heartbeat and pulled at her breath.

As the wind swung round she felt the warm breath of the South Wind on her skin and clung to her last vestige of hope.

The West Wind set her down and she turned to the South. "Please. Can you help me?"

He circled her and wrapped her in his warmth, and she felt the dry air of the desert like silk on her skin. She breathed in the heat of him, summer days, melted snow, pollen and perfume from a thousand flowers.

"You can still go back. I can take you back. It is not

too late. Though he will be angry." He whispered the words so quietly in her ear.

"I can never go back until I have finished my task. Can you take me to him?"

"No."

"Then take me to the North Wind."

"If that is where you truly wish to go."

"Do you think," she asked, her voice little more than a sob and almost lost in the rising of the wind, "do you think he can take me to my love?"

"He is the oldest. He is the One Wind. He can go where he will and nothing can stop him, not stone, not mountains. He will know how to go to where you wish. Whether you will wish to go with him, I cannot say. Now come. Time is short and he who waits has little patience."

As they neared the home of the North Wind they flew over mountains and the hot South Wind sucked up snow behind him, warm air gathering and lifting the moisture. Then he stopped and set her down. "I can go no closer, for we never meet. Even here may be too close."

She felt around her a great disturbance in the air, a crackling, almost visible. Around her was an exaggerated brightness. Turbulent clouds were building to a storm overhead, higher and higher, a weight of water rising, pushing upwards. She felt the warm kiss of the South Wind gentle on her cheek and then he was gone. Around her thunder began to shake the sky, lightning crackled and sparked in the building clouds.

He came with the stealth of a gentle wind-cat, creeping, then a column of snowflakes built into a form. He was made of light and yet she could not see him. "You are so small, so fragile, to have come so far. Reach out your hand that I may touch you."

The voice came from all around her, familiar, caressing. She reached out her hand and felt the touch of him.

He took her hand in his and the ground fell away beneath her as she felt herself growing taller, taller, like Alice in Wonderland, until she stood face to face with him. Still she could not truly see him, though shapes formed and failed before her eyes.

"I cannot see you still," she said and he replied, "Look with your heart and your soul."

At the back of her mind a voice, a memory, whispered, "Trickster. Do not trust him."

She closed her eyes. Cold eyes. He was the merest breeze, too gentle to stir a blade of grass at that moment but he carried a deadly cold.

She opened her eyes. He was made of light and ice, and she saw the face of her father melt into the face of her mother and then her love, and all around him the bear.

Only the hand of the great North Wind saved her from falling as she saw for the first time in years the face of her love, and he was more beautiful than she ever remembered, white and shimmering, now bear, now man. She reached out to touch his face and he kissed her open hand.

Then he was gone again and behind her the North Wind breathed soft on the back of her neck. Her hand burned with the cold kiss.

Again he was there. "What do you wish for?" His voice was like cracking ice on water.

She tried to pull her senses back together. Her heart raced as she watched his face change from man to bear and back again. Fascinated. Hypnotised.

He smiled.

"Trickster," La Baragouin had said. "He can take whatever shape is dearest to your heart."

"I think you know what I want. I think you know what I seek. Can you take me there?"

For a second his eyes hardened. He settled into the shape of the bear.

"I can take you there, if you still wish to go. But first I have things to show you."

"And then will you take me there?"

"If you still wish to go. But first you must hear, and listen well, for I too have waited for you, watched you and followed you. I will take you but I will have payment. Will you give me what I ask?"

"I will do anything to get to my love."

"We will see," said the wind, and he flickered back to the shape of the man with the dark eyes, but now instead of pools of sorrow they were pools of light.

"Trickster, trickster." The words sang at the back of her mind like a distant echo from long ago.

"I have watched you as you travelled, and I have seen you grow from a girl into a beautiful woman, strong and brave. And I know that you have felt me watching you. I was the wolf and the lynx and the bear, I saw you through the eyes of the red fox and the vulture. I kissed your cheek and stroked your skin and drew you ever closer. Everything you have ever done, every step you have taken has been to bring you here to me now. And now I ask you. Put down your task and stay with me – don't speak, only listen. Wait. Watch."

He took his hand away from her and stepped back. She felt unnerved, unsure. The look he gave her was a look of hunger.

She turned away, but the movement of his hand drew her eyes back. As he moved his hand over the fabric of her red dress it took on the feel of heavy silk. Patterns began to grow in the red. Frost-stitched, white flowers with delicate intricacy. Around her neck he placed a ring of hailstone, cold pearls built around hearts of fine pollen. As it touched her turquoise necklace she felt the warmth drain away from the bone-white bear.

In the castle East of the Sun and West of the Moon the prince turned in a troubled dream, cold to his bones, and he shivered.

The North Wind smiled.

He raised a collar of ice high around the back of her neck, finest lace, and on her head a crown of snowflakes threaded through with filaments of moon-gold. So light.

"Stay with me, stay with me. Forget your man who sits and waits in his tower in the castle. He has nothing for you. Stay with me and be my Snow Queen. See. Look. How beautiful you are." He held up a sheet of the purest ice as a mirror for her to see.

Into the ice she looked. The last time she had looked into a mirror was when she had visited her family that Christmas so very long ago. Then she was a girl, so young. Now she stood before the North Wind, dressed like a queen and she could see that she was indeed a woman. It was as if a stranger looked back at her. Skin pale with cold, spare of flesh but strong, hair wound and bound in ribbons of ice, pearls sparkling round her neck and a crown of snowflakes, lips cold blue. She was the Snow Queen.

He gave her time enough to wonder and look, then pulled her close to him. "Now, see what I can give you."

He took her in his arms and they flew, high into the air, where their flight made a halo round the sun. Over the clouds they went, until the world was small beneath them and they could hear the music of the stars, then down towards the cold sea.

She watched as the Northern Lights danced a crown across the ice for her. Ice sheets changed from purple to gold to turquoise and peacock blue, then back again to gold, and she had never seen such purity of colour.

The Wind calmed and slowed and came to rest. He set her down on a raised hill of ice. "Why do you love him? He who sits and waits?"

She thought. Her mind was dazzled by the beauty, of herself, of the world around her. "I love his gentleness. His kindness."

"That was not him," said the Wind. "That was the bear. For one night only you saw him. One night, and now you spend your life trying to find him. One night. It is not the man you love. It is the bear."

She thought again of his dark eyes, of his gentleness, of his rich, yellow-white, deep, thick fur.

"Stay with me. Stay with me and I will make you Queen of the White Bears." He swept his arm around, and there before her on the ice she could see one thousand great white bears, beautiful, wild and fierce.

She drew in breath and the cold touched deep in her soul. Fingers reached for her heart. Over her hands ice-lace cuffs fell and ice gold spun patterns across her skin.

The North Wind looked at her and smiled. Then, over the bears he carried her, he himself shaped like a giant bear, and all the wild bears below bowed down before her on the ice, and the Northern Lights coloured the sky with glory, for her.

He had sculpted the ice into beautiful shapes, the better to catch the colour of the light, for her. He took her to where the white wolves howled, making their music for the moon, and for her. He called a white falcon out of the sky to sit on her hand, and flew with her through flocks of swans, white wings whistling their sky music, only for her.

Over land and sea, North, South, East and West, he carried her in his arms, to where the white whales gather to sing in the water, to where the dark whales throw themselves from the sea to the air, leaping for joy and for freedom.

He showed her a world of wild beauty, cranes dancing in a snow storm, white hares dancing in the moonlight. Then he set her high on a palace of ice above a sea of ice and waited.

Never had she felt so alive, so touched by the beauty of the world. He became a breeze and moved around her, stroking her cheek, brushing her hand, then her lips, the back of her neck.

"Why do you love him?" His voice was a sigh.

"A thousand years he waited for me."

"And I have waited since the beginning of time. I have seen you wake and walk through forest, mountains, woods and deserts and I have watched you and drawn you ever closer. From the beginning of time, when I carried the first sound around the world and spread seeds to grow over the face of it, I have waited for you. I have shaped you, carved your face as I carve rock, my hand has sculpted you. Stay with me. Be my queen and I will show you what love is."

She felt the weight of the ice stitched into her dress. She felt it in every place where it lay upon her skin. She looked at the Wind as his shape changed and shimmered and she knew that she could love him.

For the first time since the beginning of her journey she saw a different path. "I have no choice." Even as she spoke the lie she knew it for what it was. "I am part of his story."

The wind knew now that he was winning. "You always have choice. And you have courage. Live your own story and step out of his. Come live with me and be my queen. I can bend and break the tallest tree, carve rock or ice, build ocean waves to sweep across the world. Or I can carry a whisper across the desert to charm an ear, and be the gentlest lover."

All the while he swirled gently round her with a touch like wings, and she leaned towards his touch and his fingers moved ever closer to her heart.

"Hold out your hand." Into her hand he dropped a perfect, delicate, white flower. Anemone. La Baragouin had said he had no heart. She was wrong. "Let him wait in his tower. Let him wait with his Troll Queen. What can he give you? You can choose. Be his wife. Be my queen."

But with these words he lost. Her heart had almost turned to ice, but now it cracked like ice in a thaw. She felt warmth returning to her face, her lips turned red and blood that had frozen began to move again, as she thought of him waiting, watching and waiting for her to come, day after endless day, to the end of time and the ends of the earth. A promise.

The white flower fell from her hand.

"I choose. I will be no one's wife and no one's queen. My story is tangled with his, for now. I have travelled far to find him and I will finish it. Then I will choose which path to follow. You offer me so much. You flatter me with your words, you lay the world at my feet. I could love you, oh, I could, for you are wild and free, beautiful and powerful. And yet you hide behind a mask, an image of my love, my man, my bear. Why do you not show yourself as you are?"

As her heart warmed, she began to feel the North Wind. He was jealous, angry at his own stupidity. His arrogance had led him to bring to her mind her love in his castle tower, waiting for her, and now he had lost her. She had slipped through his fingers. For now.

"I could freeze you to a statue, keep you here forever, young and beautiful."

"But you won't." Even as she spoke she felt her skin begin to stiffen with a skin of ice. "You could take my heart, but it would be a dead heart. You cannot take love, it has to be given."

"You want him, then go to him. See what he can give you. It is not the man you love, but the idea of love itself. Go on. Go."

His voice blasted her with a cold that bit into her skin and into her bones, but she stood her ground. "I cannot get there without your help. You know that. You alone know where the castle lies. You alone have the strength to take me there. I ask now, for the sake of love, will you take me there?"

Her words fell into stillness.

Then a sigh, and the Wind replied. "Not alone. I can take you, but you must help me. Now we will see how strong your love is. Will you do anything I ask in order to reach him?"

"Yes."

"If you falter you will fail. If you refuse I will not have the strength to carry you. Two things."

"Ask."

"The first. A kiss."

She thought for a moment, only a moment. Already she knew she loved this strange creature that was the wind. She had felt it even as his fingers crept towards her heart, as if it cleft her heart in two.

Her love for the bear had been small compared to this. The bear had needed her, he had been kind, magical, the young man beautiful, his story sad. On her journey she had grown. She loved him no less, but the North Wind was magnificent. He did not need her, but he wanted her. With him she felt beautiful, powerful, invincible. She thought of Chloris. One kiss. There could be no harm in that.

"Yes."

But there was harm, and passion, cold passion that she had never known before, that left her senses reeling.

"And now, the cloak you wear is tied with a wind-spell."

Still her thoughts were scattered. A wind-spell, yes, and he was a trickster with no heart. The first for a breeze, the second a strong wind.

"Undo the third knot."

Her hand went to the spell. "Never," La Baragouin had said. "Trickster," she had called him. "He will try to steal your heart because he has none." And yet, when she had kissed him she had felt a heartbeat that led back to the beginning of the world, had heard music from the dawn of time, had felt her life spread across the universe, had touched the stars.

She shook her head to clear her thoughts. Her fingers moved to the knot. "Why?"

"There is only one way to reach the castle and, strong as I am, I need the help of the wind-spell. Only you can undo it. It will not work for me. It was given to you. Only if you have the courage to trust me and to unleash the spell will you ever see him."

He spun around her, restless, yearning, radiant with light and took the form of her love, the bear with the man's face pale behind it, and for a moment she thought she could see his true image hidden behind the mask.

She could stay here in this moment, she could be the Snow Queen, beloved of the North Wind with power beyond her dreams.

She could undo the third knot and hurl herself towards destruction or salvation.

Cold fingers fumbled, the Wind groaned and the groan moved towards a roar. Loss and rage and power built as the cord loosened and the knot came free. She felt herself falling, falling, shrinking, sickening and dizzy, to the size of a linnet, and then as if she was slammed into a wall of rock he picked her up like a leaf in a gale and she flew.

No time to catch breath, conscious, not conscious, moving through time and space, blown by the Wind, by a force, by a power to the sound of a thousand beating wings.

How long they flew she did not know, but they came to a place where all movement ceased and he put her on the earth where she stood, shaking. He drifted away, a short distance. He seemed smaller, weakened, almost stripped of his glamour.

From the small distance he looked at her. The ice patterns had melted from her clothes as he set her down on the barren earth. Her dress hung ragged and heavy with water. The hail pearls had fallen, ripped from her neck as they flew, and the crown of gold and snowflakes had scattered to the four corners of the world. Her face was marked with sharp scars where the ice tears had cut. She was wretched, exhausted.

He shook his head. "Whatever happens now, remember this. I know your name, Berneen."

The words were a gentle breeze, a trick of the wind, a sigh. So much love in them, more than she had ever felt before.

So long had it been since she had heard her name spoken, and now here and by him. The words were a spell.

He turned and walked away and she thought she heard an ice tear falling from his eye.

For a long time Berneen stood. Hope had fallen away with the melting of the crown. She had fallen for the sweet words of the trickster and let him dazzle her with his charm and glamour. She had been entranced. He had filled her head with wonder until she had betrayed herself and kissed him and then who had untied the knot.

She had seen the devastation of the Wind as they flew over the world, ancient trees ripped from the earth, roofs peeled from house, ships pulled from their moorings and crashed onto rocks. He threw things around as an angry child throws toys. Whole forests lay flattened because of her, because she had untied the knot. And he had tricked her at the last because she had rejected him, and taken her to this barren rock at the end of the world.

All was lost.

There was no castle East of the Sun and West of the Moon. She was mad. She had loved him, the North Wind, full of power and wonder. He had tricked her. Heartless. He had left her here to die.

She sank to her knees. Why had she trusted him? Why did she ever think that he would take her to her love when she had refused to be his queen? Why had she not heeded the warning of the wise La Baragouin?

She threw back her head to the sky and howled a wild and mournful cry to the stars. Primitive. Desperate.

Here on this barren rock with the sea at one side, she saw the full moon hang over the water. Behind, she felt the first touch of the sun and turned to see the sky begin to lighten. The moon was lit from below and the whole sea shone with silver light, soft, radiant. One by

132

one the stars began to disappear until only Orion the Hunter showed bright.

Then, as day and night tipped to a perfect balance and moon-shadows melted with the light of the sun, the walls of the castle appeared. Here, in this moment where day and night met, was the castle. And at this moment she knew that she loved the North Wind, because he had brought her to this place.

The moon slid gently into the sea and daylight coloured the sky and the castle walls. She put out her hand to catch one perfect snowflake. Then all was stillness.

The walls of the castle were high. There was no door that she could see. She walked all around and found no way in.

So she sat down to rest in the warm sun beneath the castle wall and took from her bag the golden apple, that smelled so sweet, and began to throw it up and catch, throw it up and catch, up and catch, up and catch. The apple caught the sunlight and made golden patterns dance on the castle walls.

Above her she heard a window creak open, and a voice called down.

"You, girl."

A voice like the sea rolling pebbles on the beach.

"Yes." Up and catch and the golden patterns danced.

"What price for your golden apple?"

The scent of the apple travelled up to the window in the still air, sweet as if fresh-picked that moment from a golden tree.

"I've heard tell that within these castle walls lives a dark-eyed man from far, far away."

"Yes." The voice of the troll crashed down like falling rock.

"One night alone with the dark-eyed man. That is my price." She caught and held the apple and looked up. "Then you may have the apple for your own."

"Done." The window slammed shut above her.

All day she waited in the hot sunshine, nervous with excitement. Would he still know her? She had been through so much. Would he still want her? He had waited so long.

Time slowed. A day had never been so long. The sun drew its path across the cloudless sky. Not a breath of wind. The air was sharp and clear, like air before a storm. The scent of the apple in her hand was warm and heady. There was no other scent in this windless place. No wind to bring life, not a tree, no flower or blade of grass. No birds. Nothing.

But from time to time the memory of the North Wind blew around her mind and she would smile.

In the early evening light, the low slant of the sun revealed a door in the castle wall.

The Troll Queen's daughter came herself to let the

girl in. She looked her over and the girl looked back. They were rivals. There was something uncanny in the way the troll looked. She bore a remarkable resemblance to Berneen. Long dark hair. Her clothes were similar. She eyed the girl as if to steal every detail of her. Her eyes were amber, cold. Cat's eyes. She snatched the apple and led her through the castle where shadowy figures moved, around corners, behind curtains, to the room in the castle tower.

As she walked through the door, the troll caught her arm. "One night and one night only. In the morning it's out of the castle for you."

The girl stepped into the room and the heavy door swung closed behind her and she thought she heard a laugh like breaking rock from the other side.

The stillness in the room was heavy. She stood at the door as her eyes settled to take in the dim light. Her heart hammered hard in her breast.

Lanterns hung from the ceiling, tiny star-shaped lanterns, and each glowed with the small, warm light of a candle. There was a hush, not a movement, not a sound but for the steady moth-breath of a sleeping soul.

He lay in the bed in a deep sleep, lost to the world in a dream of flying in a star-filled sky, along a pathway of starlight. Across the floor she stepped lightly, the last steps of her long, long journey. She stood, an arm's reach away, a kiss away. Still he slept. She leant over him, closer and closer, reached out her hand to touch his pale face. So lost in sleep, he did not feel how near she was, how close. Close enough to feel the warmth of him.

"I have come," she said, "across the world, and I have found you." The words were a whisper, so as not to startle.

He did not hear.

She brushed his face with her hand. Still he did not wake. She lightly kissed his face, light as the brush of a butterfly's wings. Then his lips. Not even the flicker of an eyelid. Fear began to prick at her skin. She shook his shoulders.

Nothing.

With two hands now she shook him, but still he lay as if dead. Fear strangled her heart and she put her ear to his mouth. She could hear him breathe, feel the warmth of him on her skin. She shouted, she shook, she wept and she railed against the world, but nothing would stir him from his prison of sleep.

All night she wept tears of despair, frustration, sorrow. To have come so close, so very close, and still to look failure in the face. She lay beside him on the bed and held his sleeping head and washed his face with her tears until sleep took her too.

As the first fingers of sunlight crept into the room the Troll Queen's daughter opened the door. She was led away, down the stairs and out of the castle, where the door slammed shut behind her.

Tired and sick and dizzy, she leant against the castle wall. So close, so close. She had held him and he had slept, as if spelled into the deepest sleep. Not even her love or a kiss could wake him.

As light flooded into the day she looked around at the barren wasteland where the castle stood. White glowed from the ground. Where the North Wind had walked away from her only yesterday, when she still had hope, anemones had grown in his footsteps, in this barren place.

She smiled to see the white flowers, and the faintest

movement of air brought their sweet perfume to her, a
gift from the Wind.

Underneath the castle wall she took out of her bag the
golden carding comb and began to pull it through her
wind-twisted, tangled hair. As she combed, small seeds
of grass and wild flowers fell about her, stitched through
her hair by the wind's hand. And she smiled as she
thought of him, so strong, but carrying these delicate
seeds of life to spread beauty around the world.

Her hair became smooth, shining in the sun. She
took out some wool and began to card, pulling and
combing, pulling and combing until it changed from a
stiff, coarse wool to the smoothest fibres, ready to spin.
As she combed she sang. Light flashed on the gold of
the comb and made patterns dance on the castle walls.

Above her head a window opened. "Still here?"

She pulled and combed, pulled and combed, teasing
the wool and sang. The light from the golden comb
flashed and tempted.

"What price for your golden carding comb?" The voice like shattered rock.

"One night alone with your dark-eyed man in the starlit room in the castle."

"Done." The window slammed shut above her.

In the heat of the day she slept a little, but woke all too soon with the sun still high in the sky and the long wait until evening ahead.

Was he ill? Why could she not wake him? Was he bewitched? Why could she not wake him with a kiss? In stories it always worked. She thought of Snow White and her prince, Sleeping Beauty in her tower. Why would it not work for her? Was it because her heart was not pure enough, her love not strong enough? She pulled and tugged and worried at her problem as she pulled the comb through the wool, but while the wool became smooth and silky her problems remained tangled.

Then it was evening and the low slant of light made visible the castle door, and again the Troll Queen's daughter came to take her to the room. This time she was almost a mirror image of Berneen. A glamour flickered around the troll like light on a dragonfly's wings. Her hair, her skin, her face, her clothes. So like they could be twins. She walked behind the girl and watched the way she moved, head high and proud. Around them shadowy figures went about their work, bowed down by servitude, lost in the darkness, prisoners in the castle.

At the tower door the troll took the golden comb. "Hush now." Gravel voice. "Mind you don't wake him." Cold, amber eyes, narrow slits of black. She laughed, and closed the door, and Berneen could hear laughter like raining pebbles as the troll moved away down the tower stairs.

In the room alone with him all was as it had been before. He slept, and try as she might, nothing would wake him.

The lanterns hung from the ceiling. By his bed a cup, empty now, and the shirt, the white shirt, three drops of candlewax marring its purity, hung on the wall by the bed.

As she looked around the room she saw that it was full of paintings. Paintings of her. Everywhere she looked, paintings of her walking, through forests, in mountains, across deserts, riding on the back of the white bear, walking beside him through an avenue of winter trees. Opposite the bed was a mirror image of the painting from her home of the girl sleeping with the bear on the bed of leaves. On a table by the window, paints, paper, jars of pigments, beautiful colours, brushes and glass and a grindstone.

All the time he had been waiting for her to come he had painted and coloured her image. The Troll Queen's daughter had watched, seen the love with which he stroked the paint to pull her face out of the paper, to bring her ever closer. She had glamoured herself to look like the girl in the paintings, the girl in his heart, so that he would love her.

He knew nothing of the pain it caused as she pulled her sharp teeth back into her head to mould her features to be like the girl in the painting, how she compressed her stone flesh, the agony as her claws drew in to make hands as soft and gentle as the hands in the painting, how she straightened her back, smoothed her rock skin.

He knew nothing, and even if he did he would have cared less. As every day and week and month and year passed he only painted more, refusing to accept her, refusing to see how she made herself for him, to be like his love. For him.

As Berneen looked at the paintings and felt the love in every brush stroke, she wept to think of him waiting. She wept for herself, for her feeling of powerlessness. And she wept for the troll, the amber-eyed troll, who loved him also but could not make him love her back. In the tower with the sleeping prince, Berneen wept tears of sorrow for the troll, whose heart was breaking too.

In the room beneath, a servant girl heard the sound of weeping in the tower, and in the morning she watched through a crack in the door as the dark-haired woman from the prince's paintings was taken down the stairs and out of the castle.

A long day ahead and one more chance. Three women had given her three gifts, and said she would know how to use them and when. Now she began to wonder if she had used them in the right way. She had made mistakes before. She had lit the candle that her mother had given her. Maybe what she did now was wrong. Maybe she was squandering her gifts. How could it be that anyone could sleep so deeply?

She was so tired.

Out of her bag she took the beautiful spinning wheel, so delicate, so intricate with its many-coloured gold, treadle and maiden, flyer and whorl, wheel and axle. In the sun, by the wall she sat and began to spin the wool she had carded the day before, and into the thread she spun the hair she had combed as she untangled the pattern of the wind from it.

After a while she realised that the barren landscape around her was changing. The white anemones still blossomed and their faint perfume hung in the still air. Now, all around where she had sat and combed grasses grew, small shoots greening the earth.

She sat, and spun, and thought of the Wind. How

he carried life all around the world, how he stroked like a cat, roared like a lion. How he planted seeds and brought great giants of trees crashing to the ground.

The wheel turned, hypnotic, and her thoughts turned with it. The thread she spun with the wool and the hair was the finest. The golden wheel flashed patterns of light on to the tall castle wall. Around her, thistledown lifted in the almost still air, hanging and falling as the wheel turned and the Wind whispered an almost imperceptible love song. The gold coloured the castle wall.

Above her a window opened and the troll's gravel voice fell down to her. "You. Girl."

Berneen continued spinning, singing, soft voice mingling with the hush of the wind sending light spinning around her, the wheel like a small sun, a fallen star.

In her tower the troll hated her.

"What price for your spinning wheel?" The words tumbled down like rocks from a cliff.

Inside her head Berneen struggled to find another way. This was her last chance. She had to be sure.

But there was no other way that she could see. If it was her last night then she would spend it with him. Somehow she would wake him, or find a way to let him know that she had come, had not forgotten or forsaken him.

"One night with the dark-eyed prince and you can have the wheel."

"Done."

For the rest of the day she sat by the wall, the wheel idle. She watched the grass grow, small flowers mixing with the green. Forget-me-not, blue jewels in the green.

When evening came the troll opened the door. Now the resemblance was almost perfect. She wore the same clothes. Her long dark hair was combed to silk. She took the spinning wheel from Berneen and as she did it faded a little, lost something of its shine. She led her through the castle corridors to the tower, opened the door and pushed her in.

As she slammed the door behind her she said, "Tomorrow we are to be married, the dark-eyed prince and I, so be sure you do not tire him. Let him sleep."

Her laugh rolled around the room like rocks in a landslide.

In the room lit with stars and strewn with paintings he lay as if dead in the huge bed, eyes closed tight against the day.

She walked across the room, heavy heart, unsure. She did not even try to wake him. He looked so still, so peaceful. She lay down beside him, head on the pillow next to his head. What could she do to wake him from this deep, dark sleep? Above her the tiny lanterns shone their warm glow around the room. For a moment, just a moment, she could pretend that all was well, they were alone in the world together. No troll, no castle, no wedding tomorrow.

She felt so tired, so very tired, a weariness that ran through her bones, her blood, her heart and her soul. A tear filled each eye and ran down the soft scars left by her ice tears.

He reached a hand across the bed and took her hand in his, warm and lovely. With his other hand he brushed away the tears. She almost screamed, but he held her close and put his finger to her lips and whispered, "Shush now, she must not know that I am awake. If she knew she would kill me."

She tried to be quiet. Relief flooded through her and she lay in his arms so close, and he was awake. At last, journey's end.

"But how? Why now? Two nights I have been here. Two nights I have tried to wake you and each night have been taken away in the morning." She tried not to think of what would happen the next morning when the troll princess found them.

"Today, when the servant girl came to help with my paints she told me how, for the last two nights, she had heard a woman weeping in my room. She said the woman came at sunset and left at sunrise. This morning she peeped through a crack in the door and saw, she said, the woman from my paintings made flesh. Each evening the troll princess has brought me a drink, to ease my troubled mind, she said. To drug me into a sleep from which nothing could wake me. I did not usually sleep well. The dark nights were so long without you. So this night I only pretended to drink, pretended to sleep, and waited."

Berneen smiled. So much relief. So long a journey. He was every bit as beautiful as she remembered.

All night they talked in hushed whispers. He held her back at arm's length, the better to see her.

"I have changed so much." Suddenly she felt shy.

"You have grown. When I left you were a girl and now you are a woman." His fingers traced the scars on her face, scars which made her no less beautiful. "How did you find me?"

"I followed my heart," she said simply.

A leaf tap-tapped on the casement window. In the room downstairs the servant girl wept silently.

She told him of her journey, the three women and the winds that had carried her. She did not tell him how the North Wind had wooed her, only that his strength had carried her here when none other could.

He told her of his waiting, day after day, knowing she would come. How he passed each day painting, trying to hold the image of her in his mind's eye. How every day the troll princess had come and looked at the paintings and every day had tried to grow more like her. But he did not tell her of the pretty serving girl who helped him every day to grind the pigments and mix his paints to make the pure colours, and how her company eased his loneliness.

They lay together, lost in the moment, afraid of the future.

An hour before dawn he whispered of the wedding. "She has grown tired of waiting. In the morning we are to be wed. I have only one chance to escape and you have come just in time. I can set a task, for her, for you. Whoever succeeds can be my bride."

Her heart sank. Another task, and she was so weary.

"The shirt that hangs by my bed has three drops of candle-wax, from your mother's candle. I will say that I wish to wear it for my wedding shirt. I will ask both of you to wash it. Whoever washes it clean will be my wife.

"But we must beware. As a child, if she could not have something that she wanted, she would break it, smash it into a million pieces. If she cannot have me she may kill me."

"She has waited for you for so long. She too must love you very deeply, in her own way."

"All my life she has held me prisoner. She has shaped herself the best she can to look like you, so that I will love her. But she is not able to see that you cannot force someone to love you, you cannot lock them in a cage and expect them to love you back."

"Her poor heart must ache, for she must know that."

"Her 'poor' heart is black and dark and made of stone." His voice held a world of bitterness.

But Berneen knew what it was like to feel her heart ache in her breast for the one she loved, and she could not help but feel sympathy for the Troll Queen's daughter and her lonely passion.

They talked in quiet whispers through the night, wrapped in each other, close. Inside, her feelings flew around like leaves in a gale. Just before the sun came up they drifted into shallow sleep, arms around each other, his head on her shoulder, her hand on his heart.

This was how the Troll Queen's daughter found them, and inside her heart rage and jealousy and hatred burned.

$\mathcal{T}$hey were taken together to the Great Hall where the Troll Queen sat on her high throne of granite. The hall was decked in white for a wedding. Around the walls people stood and watched, servants of the troll, lost people from every nation, the missing, snatched by the Troll Queen to work forever as slaves, now to be guests at the fake wedding.

The prince stood with the two who loved him by his side. The serving girl carried his white shirt like a baby in her arms. In front of them a great tub of water. They could have been twins, Berneen and the Troll Princess, but for the amber eyes of the troll and the two scars on Berneen's face. The troll had thought them imperfections and had failed to see that they were part of what made this woman truly beautiful. From the corner of her amber eyes she watched them still, the dark rage of hatred seeping out from her heart now, around her body through her blood.

At first she had stood and watched the two sleeping,

so wrapped in each other, peaceful, beautiful. Tears had come as she knew that she could never have this, waking with him in the soft morning light.

Then she had felt the rage build, had crashed to the bed and torn the girl from his side by her hair, had been about to smash her face into the wall, to break her bones, to crush her skull. Berneen hung helpless from the troll's hand.

He had thrown himself at the troll's feet and on his knees had begged her to stop, and somehow his words had calmed her rage. He had said that he would marry her, if only she would stop, but never, never if she harmed this feeble, scarred thing.

But then he had said that he wanted to wear the shirt in his room as his wedding shirt. He wanted to wear the shirt with the candlewax, and he had set a task. He wanted them both to wash the shirt, to clean away the wax, and whoever could wash it clean he would willingly marry and promise to give his heart too.

She would try first. It could not be so difficult. He would give his heart willingly. She could cast this rag doll out to die of sorrow outside the castle walls or wander the world and weep, knowing she had lost him. She would still have her wedding, but he would be a willing groom and he would come to see. Was she not as beautiful as this frail thing? Was she not a thousand times stronger?

Now, here in the hall, she took the shirt from the serving girl, the soft, white shirt, pure as fresh-fallen snow, with the three drops of hard wax marring its beauty. She put it into the tub of water. Even as it touched the water an inky blackness spread from her hands, creeping over the shirt, making it first charcoal, then stained to a midnight black. She pushed it under the water to hide it and panic began to rise. The wax spread and the shirt began to stiffen and crackle and the more she scrubbed the darker it became.

With a scream, she dragged the wax-heavy, wet thing from the water and flung it into Berneen's face. "Let her try. The thing is bewitched."

Berneen stepped up to the tub, shirt hanging like an animal pelt, heavy in her hands. She looked at the prince. It would never come clean now. But even as it touched the water the white began to spread. She did not scrub, she did not wash. She merely held it in the water until it was clean and pure white as her bear had been. The candle wax melted away. She lifted it free from the water and turned and held it up for the Troll Queen and the princess to see.

The Troll Princess screamed, the howl of an animal caught in a trap.

"It's a trick. She has something in her hands. Show me your hands."

She ran across the room, the stones cracking beneath her feet, to where Berneen stood, holding the shirt like a shield. She tore it from her, and straight away where the troll's hands touched it, the blackness began to spread.

"Show me your hands!"

The two stood there, for all the world like twins. Berneen looked into the amber eyes and watched the troll's heart breaking. She could hear a sound like frost splintering stone, she could smell the anger and the hatred. The mask that the troll had spun around herself began to splinter away and fall, piece by piece, like broken glass.

Inside, her heart grew darker and heavier. She began to swell and boil with hatred and rise to tower above Berneen. Still she held fast to the girl's hands. As the mask fell away the troll's nose grew, tusks and silver skin as hard as iron.

From a mouth filled with dagger teeth she screamed at Berneen.

"If I cannot have him, then neither will you."

Her voice was an avalanche, and the pain in each word was immense. The force of the hatred pushed Berneen to her knees as the Troll Princess grew, and pieces of her old image fell away to the floor around the girl, sharp as razors, a jigsaw image of the woman she had wanted to be.

The troll leant over and brought her true face close to the girl. The amber eyes were larger now, snake's eyes. Huge tusks curled from the dagger-toothed mouth. She whispered, for only Berneen to hear.

"You stole my true love's heart, you witch." Her breath like stone dust.

Berneen could say nothing. But the pain of the troll's frustration and loss, and years of empty love, cut through Berneen's heart like a knife, and the pity she felt for this terrible creature showed in her face.

This was too much for the troll. Poison filled her soul, flooding from her heart. She raised her anvil hand higher and higher to smash the girl away, The pressure of hatred was too much for one soul to bear and her heart burst inside her breast, spilling its poison to burn and boil. Her stone flesh cracked, her body crumbled, flesh became dust and covered the mirror pieces scattered over the floor.

There was silence in the great hall.

Covered in the dust and splinters of the princess's body, Berneen rose to her feet and turned to face the Troll Queen. "I am sorry, so sorry."

The queen did not hear. She rose up from her throne and moved across the floor to where the dust of her daughter lay. She fell to her knees and the castle walls shook. She picked up a handful of dust and let it pour through the fingers of her great clawed hand. All her life she had given her child everything she had ever wanted. It had never been enough. She had despaired to see her fall in love with a human, and even then had tried to get her daughter what she wanted. But no one can force a man to love against his will. Now it was all too late.

Great pebble tears filled her eyes and crashed to the floor. A weight of sorrow washed around the room like a tide. The death of her child was too much for the troll's heart to bear. She shattered and crumbled into a million pieces, and she too became dust at Berneen's feet. What was left of the shirt lay covered in rock dust.

Berneen felt a great sob wrack her body. The prince stepped forward to take her in his arms.

Around the walls the servants of the castle seemed to wake from a nightmare. Out of the silence a murmur began, rose to a cheer and then a roar. It was over. They were free.

Berneen seemed stunned. The prince took her back to his room in the castle tower and the serving girl helped her into bed. Soon she fell into a deep sleep, exhausted. And while she slept, the prince explored the castle that had been his prison. It was full of people stolen by the trolls from all around the world to work for them as slaves. There were rooms full of beautiful things too – paintings and jewellery, clothes and furniture.

He gathered together the people. They were free now to do as they wished. They could stay in the castle, or try to find their way home. They could take what they wanted.

In the castle kitchens he found fruit and cheese, bread and wine. He laid out a small feast and took it back to his room. He sat and watched as Berneen slept, this woman who had walked across the world to find him and free him. All day he sat, in the evening, and on through the night as the moonlight bathed her face with silver.

Outside, the wind blew a leaf to tap against the window and she stirred in her sleep and smiled, but did not wake. Then the sunlight painted the colour back into her cheeks, and still she slept, and still he waited.

When Berneen woke the sun was high in the sky. He had fallen asleep beside her on the bed. She reached across and took his hand in hers. At last they were free.

His eyes opened, half asleep, half awake. So often he had dreamt of this moment, he thought he dreamed now. Only the warmth of her hand told him she was truly here beside him.

They rose and shared the breakfast. A shyness settled on them. They talked of nothing, of the brightness of the day, of the warmth of the air. Anything except what had happened the day before. Outside a bird sang.

Berneen walked to the window and opened it wide. Below, as far as the eye could see, the earth was carpeted with a white tapestry of delicate swaying anemones. She smiled to see them.

"We can be married now, you and I." The voice came from the room behind her.

She turned and looked at the beautiful, dark-eyed prince. His eyes were no longer sad.

"No," she said. "Now you and I are free, for the first time in years. Free to live our own lives. You may do as you wish, go where you will."

"But I wish only to marry you. I love you. You love me. You made the shirt pure white again."

"Yes, I made the shirt white, I travelled the world to find you. I fell in love with you when you were a bear, and again on the night I first saw you as a man. When you were taken I thought my heart would break in two. I promised I would search until I found you, even if the search led to the ends of the earth, and I did. The road to here was a long road. I learnt many things. I grew from a child to a woman. You needed me to break the spell of the bear, and again to free you from the love of the troll. You do not need me any more.

"I promised to find you. But I do not know you, you do not know me, only the child that I was. My heart now belongs to another."

He shook his head. This was not how it was meant to be. "It can't end like this. I love you." In a small voice. "What am I to do?"

"Now you must begin to live for yourself. You could stay here and help the people of the castle. The Wind has come here and brought life. You could try to find your way back into the world. You can go where you will, be who you want to be. This is not an ending, but a beginning. Now we are both free."

Outside, the wind was rising.

She looked away again, out of the window.

"But where will you go, what will you do?"

"On my journey I followed a stream for a while, through valleys and woods. I drank from it and took silver fish from under shaded trees. It was beautiful. When we came to the edge of a desert, the water soaked into the sand. I thought the stream had come to the end of its journey. But as I watched I saw the sun and the wind lift the water out of the sand, steam rising to the air. The wind carried the water over the hot desert, high in the air, until it reached the other side. Here it lifted it up, over the hills and the mountains to turn again to water in the cold, to fall as rain, to become a different stream."

For a moment she was silent, high on the windowsill above the white flowers in the castle that lay East of the Sun and West of the Moon. Then she stood and walked across the room. She kissed the dark-eyed prince and smiled. She moved back to sit beside the window.

"He carried me here to you, though he thought he had lost me. He could have left me then and I would never have reached this place without him. I will trust my heart to him, like the stream in the desert, I will give myself to the Wind, to be with him, to go where he takes me."

There was a rush of air, a wild cry of joy from the Wind, a whistling like a thousand swans' wings in flight, and she threw herself from the window and into the wild, turbulent air, arms spread wide. Arms became wings as the Wind lifted her, higher and higher, and she became falcon, white-feathered, fierce.

In the room in the tower, the prince ran to the window and watched the beautiful white bird soar into the sky. On the windowsill a single white feather twisted in the faintest stir of breeze.

Higher and higher the North Wind lifted Berneen until the earth below was covered with a roof of cloud. In the arms of the North Wind she flew, a white falcon, her heart filled with joy, with freedom, with love.